A word from Sara Fanelli

Pinocchio was a part of my childhood: I was born and grew up in Florence, the birthplace of Carlo Collodi, and the puppet was present not just in the words of the book, but also quite literally in the everyday landscape, in the shop windows and markets. Children often sang songs and rhymes about him and sometimes I even used to put on a pointy hat and pretend I was a little puppet to my family.

When I first read *Pinocchio* as a child, I reacted against its moralistic undertones; when I read it as a grown-up illustrator I fell for the energy and surrealism of the puppet's escapades. There is a wonderful tradition of Italian artists giving the story a life in pictures; I tried to create a world that would be playful and attractive to a contemporary child yet which was also truthful to the original setting of the story in rural Tuscany.

The long-awaited finale, when Pinocchio changes from being a puppet to a real boy, has always had a bittersweet tone for me — but I hope that there is enough fantasy and colour in these pages to make the story last beyond the puppet's lifespan, to overflow into a real child's world.

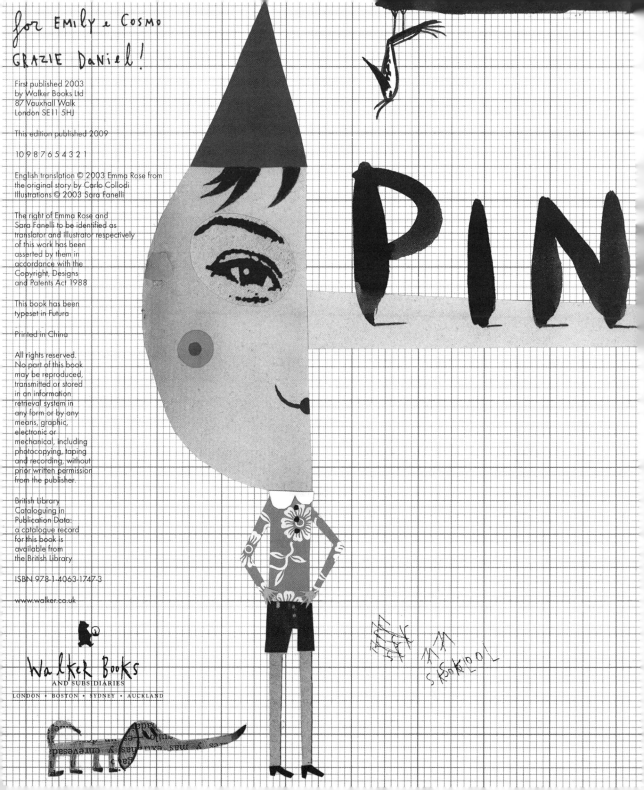

for EMILY & COSMO
GRAZIE DaNieL!

First published 2003
by Walker Books Ltd
87 Vauxhall Walk
London SE11 5HJ

This edition published 2009

10 9 8 7 6 5 4 3 2 1

English translation © 2003 Emma Rose from
the original story by Carlo Collodi
Illustrations © 2003 Sara Fanelli

The right of Emma Rose and
Sara Fanelli to be identified as
translator and illustrator respectively
of this work has been
asserted by them in
accordance with the
Copyright, Designs
and Patents Act 1988

This book has been
typeset in Futura

Printed in China

British Library
Cataloguing in
Publication Data:
a catalogue record
for this book is
available from
the British Library

ISBN 978-1-4063-1747-3

www.walker.co.uk

Walker Books
AND SUBSIDIARIES

LONDON · BOSTON · SYDNEY · AUCKLAND

PIN

OCCHIO

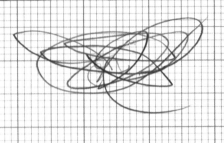

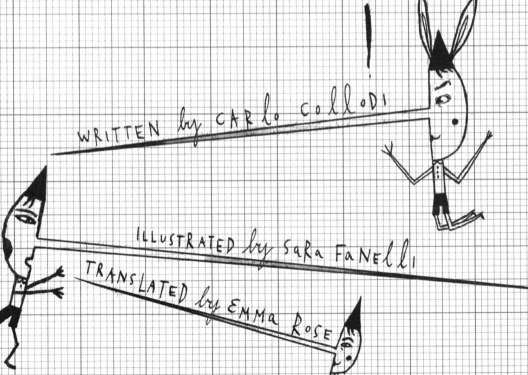

WRITTEN by CARLO COLLODI

ILLUSTRATED by SARA FANELLI

TRANSLATED by EMMA ROSE

fig. 1

fig. 2

chapter 1

Once upon a time there was...

"A king?" did I hear you cry?

But if you did cry "king", children, you were wrong. Because once upon a time there was ...

...a piece of wood.

It wasn't a piece of fine mahogany. It was an ordinary log, just like the logs you burn in your fireplace to warm your toes in winter.

Now one day this piece of wood ended up – don't ask me how – in the workshop of an old carpenter whose name was Antonio – although, on account of the tip of his nose always being red and shiny, everybody knew him as Mr Cherry.

When Mr Cherry saw our ordinary piece of wood, he was delighted.

"Perfect timing," he muttered to himself, rubbing his hands together with satisfaction. "It's just what I needed to make that table leg." And then, quick as a flash, he picked up his axe to strip the bark and whittle the wood down. But just as he was about to make the first cut, he froze with his arm mid-air. He could have sworn he'd heard a voice – a thin little voice – exclaim "Please don't hit hard!"

You can imagine how amazed Mr Cherry was.

He cast puzzled looks around the room, trying to discover where the little voice might have come from, but saw nobody. He looked under his workbench – nobody. He peered into the cupboard he always kept locked – nobody. He rummaged around in the bin he used for sawdust and wood chippings – nobody. He even opened the door of his workshop to glance down the street – still nobody. What was going on...?

"Oh well," he said to himself at last, with a laugh and a scratch of his wig. "I must have imagined it. Back to work."

He picked up the axe again, and gave the piece of wood a good whack.

"Ouch!" yelped the same little voice. "That hurt!"

This time Mr Cherry was left speechless. His eyes bulged out of their sockets. His mouth gaped open. His tongue hung down his chin. He looked like one of those stone faces you may have seen on water fountains. As soon as he got his voice back, he began talking to himself, shaking and stammering with fear. "Where on earth did that voice come from...? There's nobody here but me. Could it have been this piece of wood? Could it have learned to talk and cry like a child? No, that's ridiculous. Let's have a look at it," said Mr Cherry. "It's a perfectly ordinary kind of log. It's the kind of log that would bring your pot of beans to the boil if you threw it on the fire." Mr Cherry thought for a moment. "Is there someone hiding inside it? They'd better not be! I'll sort them out!"

And with these words he seized the poor piece of wood in both hands and began bashing it mercilessly against the four walls of the room.

Eventually he stopped, so he could listen out for more little voices. He waited for two minutes. Nothing. He waited for four minutes. Nothing. He waited for ten minutes. Still nothing.

"That's that then," he said, ruffling his wig and forcing out another laugh. "I did imagine it. Back to work."

Mr Cherry was feeling very nervous by now. He hummed a tune to encourage himself as he put away the axe and picked up a plane, meaning to smooth down the piece of wood. But when he began to run the tool along the log, he heard the little voice again.

"Stop it! That tickles!" it giggled.

This time poor Mr Cherry fell down in a dead faint. When he opened his eyes, he found himself sitting on the floor.

He'd had such a fright, his face was barely recognizable. Even the shiny red tip of his nose had turned deep blue with fear.

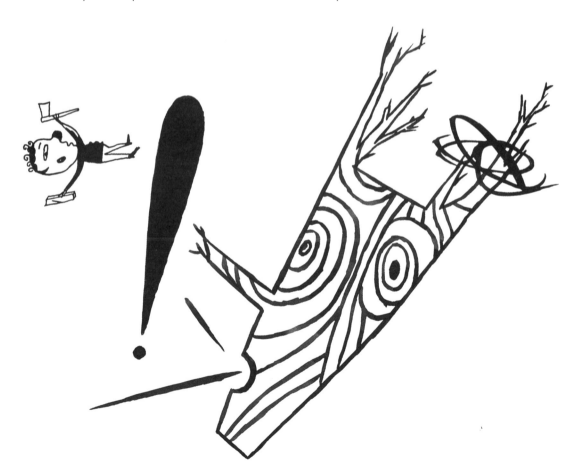

chapter 2

There was a knock at the door.

"Come in," said the carpenter, still too weak to get up off the floor.

A sprightly old man stepped into the shop. His real name was Geppetto, but when the local children wanted to tease him, they called him Maisy because his yellow wig was exactly the colour of maize porridge.

Geppetto was very short-tempered, and calling him Maisy was a good way to drive him wild. He'd fly into a rage straight away, and then there was no holding him back.

"Good day, Mr Antonio," Geppetto said. "What are you up to down there on the floor?"

"I'm teaching ants the alphabet," snapped the carpenter. "And what brought you here, Mr Geppetto?"

"My legs," Geppetto replied, to get his own back. "But seriously, Mr Antonio," he went on, "I came to ask you a favour."

"Ask away," the carpenter said, as he struggled into a kneeling position.

"I had an idea this morning," Geppetto explained.

"Let's hear it."

"I thought I'd make myself a wooden puppet. But not just any old puppet. I thought I'd make an amazing puppet. A puppet that would be able to dance. A puppet that could fence. A puppet that could do somersaults. Then I'd travel the world, showing it to the public, and earn my crust of bread that way. What do you think?"

"Great idea, Maisy!" cried the mysterious little voice that had frightened Mr Cherry earlier.

When he heard the word "Maisy", Geppetto turned bright red.

"What are you calling me names for?" he yelled at the carpenter.

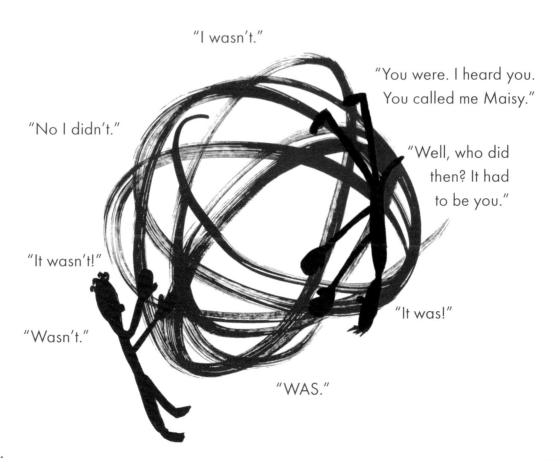

"I wasn't."

"You were. I heard you.
You called me Maisy."

"No I didn't."

"Well, who did
then? It had
to be you."

"It wasn't!"

"It was!"

"Wasn't."

"WAS."

Having worked themselves up into a rage, they moved on from words to actions and flew at each other, punching, scratching and biting.

At the end of the fight, Antonio was left with Geppetto's yellow wig in his hand. His own salt-and-pepper hairpiece was firmly clamped between Geppetto's teeth.

"Give me back my wig," said Mr Cherry.

"You give me back mine, and we'll forget the whole business."

So the two old men exchanged hairpieces, shook hands and swore they would be friends for ever.

"Now tell me," the carpenter said, as a sign that peace was restored. "What was this favour you wanted?"

"I wondered if you'd let me have a piece of wood. To make my puppet with."

Mr Cherry was delighted to help. He hurried over to his bench to fetch the log that had given him so much trouble. But just as he was about to hand it over to his friend, it jerked violently out of his grasp and landed painfully against Geppetto's bony shins. "Ouch!" cried Geppetto. "Is that how you usually give presents, Mr Antonio? You almost broke my leg!"

"It wasn't me, I swear."

"Who do you think did it then – me?"

"The log."

"I'm well aware it was the log, but you threw it!"

"I didn't!"

"Liar!"

"I'm warning you, Geppetto, I'm starting to feel like calling you Maisy..."

"Jackass!"

"Maisy!"

"Bird-brain!"

"Maisy!"

"Gorilla!"

"Maisy!"

When Geppetto heard himself being called Maisy for the third time, he saw red and leapt on the carpenter. Fists flew.

When this fight was over, Antonio had two more scratches on his nose and Geppetto had two fewer buttons on his jacket. Since this evened out the score, they shook hands and swore eternal friendship.

And Geppetto picked up his piece of wood, thanked Mr Cherry and limped off home.

CHAPTER 3

Geppetto's home was a small, dark room on the ground floor. The furniture couldn't have been simpler. There was one wobbly chair, an uncomfortable bed and a rickety table. At the far end of the room you could see a hearth with a fire burning in it. It wasn't a real fire, though – it had been painted onto the wall. Hanging over the painted fire was a painted pot, boiling away merrily and giving off a cloud of painted steam that looked just like the real thing.

As soon as he got home, Geppetto picked up his tools to carve his puppet. Suddenly he was struck by a thought.

"What shall I call him?" he wondered.

"Pinocchio is a good name," he decided. "It'll bring him luck. I knew a whole family of Pinocchios once – Mr Pinocchio, Mrs Pinocchio and the Pinocchio children – and they were all as happy as anything: the richest one begged for a living."

Now he had found a name for his puppet, he set to work from the head down, briskly carving out hair, forehead and eyes.

Once the eyes were finished, he stood back, amazed. They were moving. First they looked around a bit, then they stared at him, so intently that he felt quite put out.

"Hey! What are you looking at, you nasty wooden eyes?" he asked.

There was no reply.

Next he carved the puppet's nose. The moment it was finished, it began to grow. It grew and grew, so that in just a few minutes it was the longest nose he'd ever seen. Poor Geppetto kept trying to whittle it down, but the more he tried, the longer that mischievous nose became.

Next he carved the puppet's mouth, but it wasn't even finished before it began to laugh and jeer at him.

"Stop laughing," Geppetto snapped angrily. He might as well have been talking to a brick wall. "Stop laughing!" he shouted, "or else..."

The mouth fell silent, but stuck its tongue out instead. Geppetto thought it wise to pretend he hadn't noticed. He went on to carve the puppet's chin, neck, shoulders, stomach, arms and hands.

The moment the hands were finished, Geppetto felt something being whisked off his head. He looked up, and what do you think he saw? His yellow wig in the hand of his half-finished puppet.

"Pinocchio!" he yelled. "Give that back this instant!" The puppet did nothing of the sort. Instead he plonked the wig onto his own head, where it sank down over his eyes.

This was such insulting behaviour that Geppetto felt more miserable than he'd ever felt in his life.

"You naughty, naughty boy!" he said. "You're not even finished yet, and already you show your father no respect! I'm disappointed in you, I really am..." And as he said this he wiped away a tear.

Last of all Geppetto carved the puppet's legs and feet. The moment they were finished, he received a sharp kick on the end of his nose.

"It serves me right, I suppose," he sighed. "I should have known that would happen. No use complaining now."

He lifted Pinocchio up and stood him in the middle of the room so that he could take his first steps, but the puppet's legs were so stiff that at first he couldn't move them at all. Geppetto held him by the hand and taught him how to put one foot in front of the other.

Once his legs were loosened up, Pinocchio began to walk on his own, then to run around the room. Suddenly he made a break for the front door and began careering off down the street. Poor old Geppetto followed him, but he didn't stand a chance – the naughty puppet ran tremendously fast, in great leaps and bounds like a hare, with his hard wooden feet going clackety-clack on the cobblestones.

Geppetto was shouting "Stop him, stop him!" but, when the people on the street saw the wooden puppet flash by, they just stopped in amazement and laughed and laughed, quite unable to believe their eyes.

Luckily a passing policeman heard the commotion. He concluded that a pony must have slipped its halter, and bravely crossed the street, determined to stop the animal and avoid a dangerous accident.

Pinocchio saw that his way was barred. He tried to surprise the policeman by slipping between his legs, but the constable simply reached out a hand, caught the puppet by his ridiculously long nose (it might have been made for policemen to catch hold of) and handed him back to Geppetto.

Wanting to teach Pinocchio a lesson, the old man tried to box his ears, but couldn't find anything to box. In his hurry to make the puppet, he'd forgotten to give him any ears at all.

Shaking his head angrily, Geppetto took Pinocchio by the scruff of the neck and led him away.

"Just you wait till we get home!" he said.

When Pinocchio heard this, he flung himself to the ground and refused to budge. A crowd of curious passers-by began to gather, every one with an opinion.

"The poor little puppet!" said one. "No wonder he doesn't want to go home. That horrid Geppetto will probably give him a thrashing."

"Geppetto seems like such a nice old fellow," another added maliciously, "but with kids he's a real tyrant. If they leave that poor puppet with him, he's quite capable of smashing him to bits."

To cut a long story short, these onlookers made such a fuss that the policeman ended up freeing Pinocchio and marching his poor father off to prison. Geppetto, too shocked to argue, was crying his eyes out.

"That wicked, wicked child!" he muttered, between sobs. "And to think I tried so hard to make him a well-behaved puppet! But it serves me right. I should have known."

And so begins the extraordinary story of Pinocchio, which I will tell in the coming chapters.

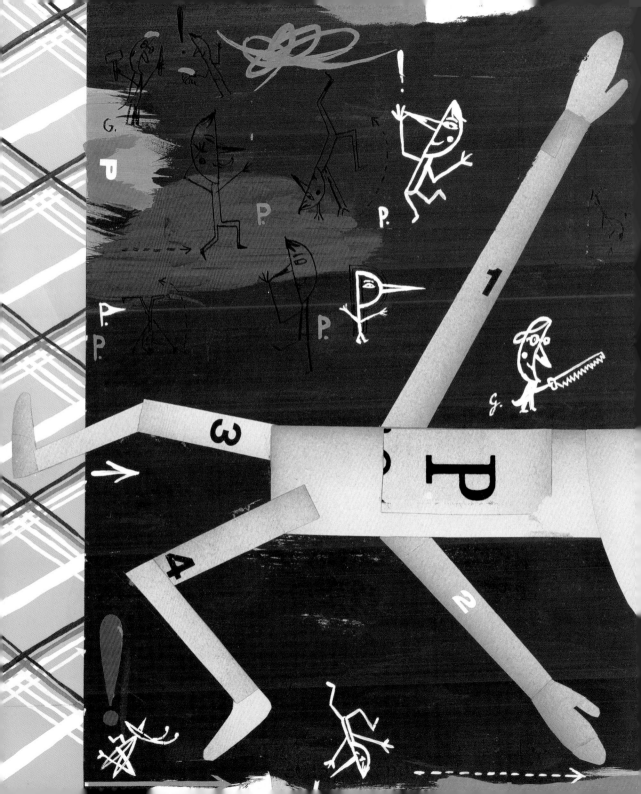

chapter 4

While poor, innocent Geppetto was being marched off to prison, Pinocchio was running home through the fields as fast as his legs would carry him. He leapt over prickly hedges and across ditches like a mountain goat or a hare running from hounds. When he reached the house, he found the front door ajar. He went in, shut the door behind him, drew the bolt and sat down on the floor with a long sigh of relief.

But his relief didn't last long. All of a sudden he heard a chirruping sound coming from somewhere inside the room.

"Who's that?" Pinocchio asked, a little frightened.

"It's me," said a voice.

Pinocchio turned round. He saw a large cricket climbing very slowly up the wall.

"And who are you?" he asked.

"I'm a talking cricket, who has lived in this room for more than a hundred years."

"Well, it's my room now," said the puppet. "So do me a favour and shove off."

"I'm not going anywhere," the cricket replied, "until I've told you one or two things about life."

"Get on with it then," Pinocchio sighed.

"Children who behave badly and run away from home will never come to any good. They'll live to regret it, sooner or later."

"Preach away, old cricket," Pinocchio said. "I don't care. At first light tomorrow, I'm off. If I stay here, I'll end up like every other child: I'll be sent to school, whether I want to go or not – and between you and me, Mr Cricket, I don't want to, not one little bit. Chasing butterflies and stealing birds' nests is much more fun."

"You stupid boy! With that attitude you'll grow up to be an ignorant ass who everyone makes fun of."

"Shut up, you horrid insect!" Pinocchio shouted.

The cricket was a patient, philosophical creature, so he didn't react. "If you don't want to go to school," he suggested calmly, "why don't you learn a trade, so you can earn your own living?"

"I'll tell you why not," snapped Pinocchio. He was beginning to get annoyed. "In the whole wide world, there's only one line of work I fancy."

"What's that?"

"Eating, drinking, sleeping and having fun. When I grow up, I want to be a professional idler."

"Bad choice," the cricket replied as calmly as ever. "That particular job is guaranteed to send you straight to hospital. Or prison."

"Don't try my patience, aged insect!"

"Poor Pinocchio, I do feel sorry for you..." the cricket sighed.

"Why?" Pinocchio bristled.

"Because you're a puppet, and because you're a blockhead."

Pinocchio leapt up furiously, seized a large mallet from Geppetto's workbench and hurled it at the talking cricket.

He may not have meant to hit him, but he did – right on the head.

The poor old insect barely had time for one last chirrup before he died, squashed flat against the wall.

CHapter 5

Night was falling and Pinocchio, who hadn't eaten yet, began to feel peckish. Young people have good appetites, and after just a few minutes he wasn't peckish any more: he was hungry. A few more minutes and he wasn't just hungry any more: he was starving – so starving he could have eaten a horse. He went straight over to the big pot that was bubbling away in the fireplace, but when he tried to lift its lid, he got a nasty surprise: the pot was painted on the wall.

Pinocchio began to run around the kitchen, rifling through drawers and store cupboards in search of something to eat: a slice of bread, a stale crust, an old bone left behind by a dog; a scrap of mouldy porridge, a fish bone, a cherry stone – anything. But there was nothing to be found. Absolutely nothing.

All the while Pinocchio was getting hungrier and hungrier. The only thing that made him feel better was to yawn. He yawned yawns so large that they almost split his face in two. After each yawn he spat, feeling as though he were spitting out his stomach.

"That cricket was right," he wailed. "I shouldn't have run away and caused so much trouble. If my father were here with me now, I wouldn't be yawning myself to death. How I hate being hungry!"

Just then he thought he saw something in the rubbish bin – something round. Something white, and very like an egg. He pounced on it immediately. It was an egg.

No words could express Pinocchio's joy, so you'll just have to imagine it for yourselves. Half afraid that he might be dreaming, he kept turning the egg over and over in his hands, showering it with kisses.

"How shall I cook it?" he wondered out loud. "Shall I make an omelette? Or would it be tastier fried? What about boiled? No, poaching is the quickest. I'm too hungry to wait." Quick as a flash, he placed a pan on a brazier of hot coals and filled it with water. When it began to boil, he held the egg over the water and cracked the shell open. But instead of the yolk and the white that he had expected, out popped a cheerful little chick. It bowed to him politely.

"Thank you so much for helping me out of my shell, Mr Pinocchio," it said. "Goodbye, and best wishes to all the family." With that, it spread its wings, flew out of the window and disappeared into the distance.

Poor Pinocchio was left standing in a daze, his mouth wide open and half an eggshell in each hand. The moment he'd recovered from the shock, he began to cry and scream. He stamped his feet in despair.

"If I hadn't run away from home and my father was here now, I wouldn't be starving to death," he wailed. "How I hate being hungry!"

His stomach was rumbling louder than ever. Since he couldn't think how else to shut it up, he decided to walk out to the nearby village, in the hope of finding some kind person who might give him a bite to eat.

CHAPTER 6

It was a grim winter's night. Great thunderclaps rolled overhead. Flashes of lightning rent the sky. A fierce wind raised great clouds of dust as it whistled angrily by, making the trees in the fields creak and groan.

Pinocchio was terrified of storms, but his hunger proved stronger than his fear. Leaving the front door ajar, he set off at top speed and reached the village in a hundred great leaps and bounds, panting and sticking his tongue out like a tired dog.

The main street was dark and deserted. Every shop was shut, every front door locked, every window tightly barred. There wasn't a soul to be seen. It was like a ghost town.

Seized by desperation, Pinocchio leant on the doorbell of the nearest house, letting it ring on and on.

"Someone will have to answer," he said to himself. Sure enough, a little old man in a nightcap leant out of an upstairs window.

"What do you want at this time of night?" he shouted furiously.

"I was wondering if you'd be kind enough to let me have a piece of bread," Pinocchio asked.

"Wait there, I'll be back in a second," said the old man, who thought he was dealing with one of those little devils who amuse themselves by dragging honest people from their beds in the middle of the night.

Half a minute later the window opened again.

"Come closer," the same old man's voice shouted down, "and hold out your hat."

Pinocchio didn't have a hat, so he just moved closer. Suddenly an enormous bucketful of water came crashing down on his head, giving him a good soaking which might have been perfectly welcome if he'd been a pot of wilted geraniums.

He got home dripping wet, exhausted and still starving. Too weak to stand, he sat down, put his muddy feet up on the burning brazier and fell asleep. Unfortunately, as he slept, his feet – which of course were made of wood – began to smoulder. They slowly crumbled into ashes, but Pinocchio just carried on snoring, as if they belonged to somebody else.

When daylight came, he was woken by a knock on the door.

"Who is it?" he asked, yawning and rubbing his eyes.

"It's me," said a voice.

It was his father.

Chapter 7

Pinocchio was still half asleep. He hadn't noticed that his feet were burnt to cinders so, when he heard his father's voice, he jumped down from his stool to go over and unbolt the door. After wobbling wildly back and forth two or three times, he came crashing to the ground with a noise like a sack of wooden spoons thrown from a fifth-floor window.

"Open the door!" Geppetto was shouting from the street.

"I can't!" the puppet wailed as he rolled around on the floor.

"Why not?"

"Because somebody has eaten my feet."

"Who has?"

"The cat," replied Pinocchio, who had just spotted the old tabby playing with some wood-shavings.

"I'll give you 'cat' when I get hold of you!" Geppetto yelled. "Open up this minute!"

"I can't stand up!" Pinocchio sobbed. "Really I can't. Oh, poor me! I'll have to walk on my knees for the rest of my life!"

Geppetto thought Pinocchio was up to his tricks again. He decided to put a stop to them, and climbed in through the window.

When he first got in, he was furious and wanted to teach the naughty boy a lesson, but when he saw poor Pinocchio lying on the floor, really and truly without any feet, his anger melted away. He lifted the puppet gently into his arms and showered him with hugs and kisses.

"My poor little Pinocchio!" he said, big tears rolling down his cheeks. "How on earth did this happen to you?"

"I don't know, Father," Pinocchio replied, "but I've had a terrible night. The kind of night a boy remembers for the rest of his life. There was thunder and lightning, and I was starving, and then the cricket said it served me right because I'd been bad, and I said, 'Watch it, cricket...' and he said, 'You're just a blockhead,' so I threw a mallet at him and he died, but it was his fault, because I didn't mean to kill him. And anyway, I put a pan on the brazier, and then this chicken came out and said, 'Goodbye, and regards to all your family,' and I was getting hungrier and hungrier, and then that old man looked out of the window and told me to come closer and hold out my hat, and then he tipped a bucket of water on my head. There's nothing wrong with asking for a piece of bread, is there, Father? So anyway, I went straight home, and I was still starving, and I put my feet up on the brazier to dry them, and you came back, and they were all burnt up, and I'm still starving, and now I don't have any feet!" And poor Pinocchio began to wail so loudly that people could hear him for at least five miles around.

From this, Geppetto had understood only one thing: his puppet was desperately hungry. He pulled three pears out of his pocket.

"These were for my breakfast," he said, handing them to Pinocchio, "but I'd rather you had them."

"If you want me to eat them, you'll have to peel them," Pinocchio replied.

"Peel them?" Geppetto repeated in amazement. "I'd never have

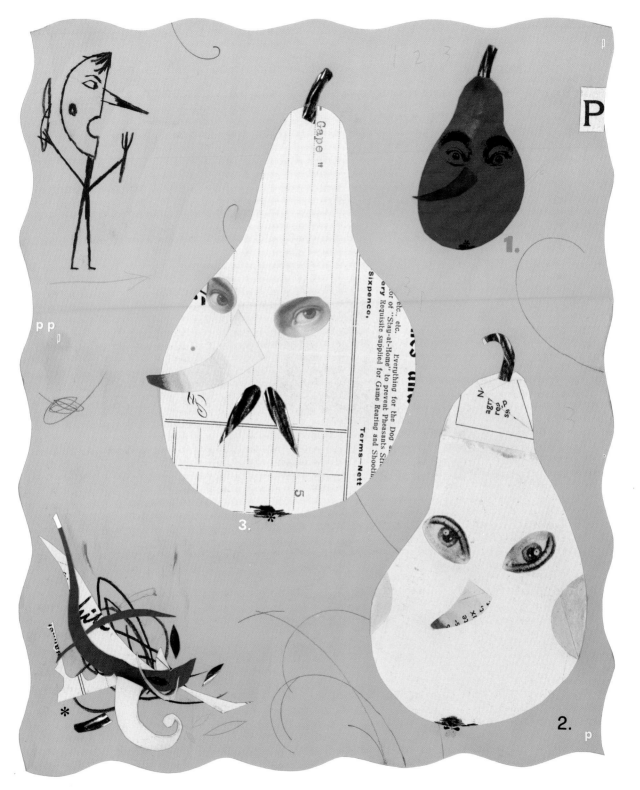

expected you to be so fussy, my boy. You must get used to eating everything, because one day you may not have any choice. You never know what might happen."

"That's all very well," Pinocchio replied. "But I'm still not eating peel. I can't stand it."

Geppetto, like the kind old man that he was, took out his pocket-knife and peeled the three pears, putting the peelings carefully to one side.

Pinocchio gobbled the first pear up in a couple of bites. He was about to throw away the core, when Geppetto stopped him.

"Don't," he said. "You might want it later."

"I don't eat cores!" the puppet shouted belligerently.

"You never know," the old man repeated patiently, "what might happen."

The three cores ended up on the table next to the peel. Once Pinocchio had eaten – or rather devoured – the pears, he gave a great yawn.

"I'm still hungry," he moaned.

"I'm afraid I've nothing else to give you, my son," his father said.

"Nothing at all?"

"Only the peel and the cores."

"Oh well," said Pinocchio. "If there really isn't anything else, I suppose I could try some peel." He began to chew on a little piece. At first he pulled a face, but in no time he'd polished it all off, and soon all the cores as well, one by one. When he'd eaten everything that was there, he patted himself on the stomach.

"That's better," he murmured contentedly.

"So you see," Geppetto observed, "I was right. You never know what might happen."

CHAPTER 8

As soon as his stomach was full, Pinocchio began to cry again, and to whine for new feet. For half a day Geppetto ignored him, to punish his bad behaviour.

Finally he asked, "And why should I make you a new pair of feet? To watch you run away again?"

"I promise I'll be good from now on," sobbed the puppet.

"That's what you children always say, when you're after something."

"I promise I'll go to school and work hard."

"That's what you children always say, when you're after something!"

"But I'm not like other children!" spluttered the puppet. "I'm better than them. I never lie! I promise I'll study, and get a job, and look after you in your old age."

Geppetto (who, despite his gruff display, was fighting back tears at Pinocchio's pitiable state) said nothing more. He fetched his tools, and two small pieces of seasoned wood, and set to work. In less than half an hour, he'd carved a pair of slim, quick little feet, as good as anything produced by a master sculptor.

"Close your eyes and sleep," Geppetto told Pinocchio. So the puppet shut his eyes and pretended to drift off.

While Pinocchio was pretending, Geppetto mixed a little glue in half an eggshell, then stuck the new feet into position. He did it so well that you couldn't even see the join.

As soon as Pinocchio realized he had his feet back, he jumped down from the table and began prancing around and turning cartwheels, as if joy had driven him quite mad.

"Thank you! Thank you! I'll go to school at once," he said to his father.

"Good boy!"

"But I can't go without clothes," the puppet pointed out.

Geppetto was poor and had no money for buying clothes, so he made Pinocchio a suit out of wrapping-paper, a pair of shoes out of bark and a hat out of a loaf of bread.

Pinocchio rushed to look at his reflection in a bucket of water. He was delighted with what he saw.

"I look like a gentleman!" he cried, striking a pose.

"You do," agreed his father. "But remember that it's clean clothes, not expensive ones, that make a gentleman."

"By the way," the puppet went on, "before I can go to school, there's one more thing I need – the most important thing of all."

"Which is?"

"A copybook."

"You're right," said the old man. "But how do we get one?"

"Easy. We go into a shop and buy it."

"With whose money?"

"I don't have any."

"Neither do I," the kind old man said sadly.

And then Pinocchio, so cheerful by nature, looked sad too, because poverty – real, grinding poverty – wears everyone down, even children.

"Never mind," Geppetto said suddenly. "It can't be helped." He pulled on his old, patched up jacket and hurried out of the house.

It wasn't long before he returned with a copybook for his son. He was in his shirtsleeves, though it was snowing outside.

"What happened to your jacket, Father?" Pinocchio asked.

"I sold it."

"Why?"

"I sold it," Geppetto replied, "because I was too hot."

When he heard this, Pinocchio's warm heart was flooded with gratitude and affection. He flung his arms around the old man's neck and showered his face with kisses.

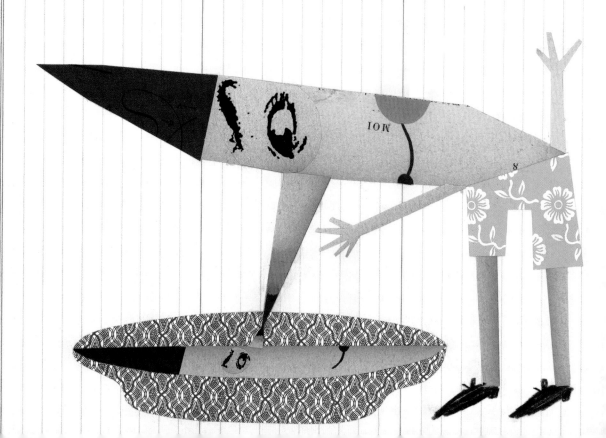

CHaPTER 9

As soon as it stopped snowing, Pinocchio set off for school, his brand-new copybook under his arm. As he walked along, his little brain built endless castles in the air, each more wonderful than the last.

"Today I'm going to learn to read," he said to himself, "tomorrow I'll learn to write, and the day after tomorrow I'll learn to do my sums. Then I'll earn lots of money, and with my very first coins I'll buy Father a smart new jacket. Not any old jacket – a silver and gold one, with jewels for buttons. After all, he's in his shirtsleeves so that I can have a book for school. And it's so cold at the moment! Only a father would do such a thing..."

Just as he was feeling deeply moved, he heard the faint sound of pipes and drums in the distance: Toot, toot, toot! Boom, boom, boom!

He stopped to listen. The music was coming from the end of a very long side-road, which led to a village by the sea.

I wonder what that is? he thought. What a pity that I have to go to school, otherwise...

He stood in the road, dithering, torn between school and music.

"I'll go and hear the music today, and start school tomorrow," he finally decided with a shrug. "There's plenty of time for learning."

And he ran off down the side-road, as fast as his legs would carry him.

The closer he got to the village, the clearer the sound of the pipes and drums became: Toot, toot, toot... Boom, boom, boom! Soon he found himself in a village square full of people crowding round a large brightly-coloured tent.

"What's in there?" Pinocchio asked a local boy.

"Read the billboard," the boy replied.

"I'd be glad to – but today, as it happens, I can't."

"Splendid! I'll read it to you then. Those bright red letters say:

GRAND PUPPET THEATRE

"Has the show started?"

"It's just about to."

"How much does it cost to get in?"

"Fourpence."

Overcome by curiosity, Pinocchio lost all sense of shame.

"Could you lend me fourpence until tomorrow?" he asked.

"I'd be glad to," the boy teased, "but today, as it happens, I can't."

"I'll sell you my jacket," the puppet volunteered.

"What use is a jacket made of wrapping-paper? If it rains, it'll stick to my back."

"What about my shoes?"

"They're only fit for firewood."

"My hat?"

"Now that really would be a bargain: a hat made of bread! It'd get eaten off my head by mice."

Pinocchio was desperate to see the puppets. He did have one last thing to sell, but he couldn't quite bring himself to do it. He hesitated. He wavered. He agonized.

"What about this brand-new copybook?" he said at last.

"I'm a child, and I don't buy anything off other children," answered the boy, who had a little more sense than our wooden friend.

"I'll give you fourpence for it," interrupted a rag-and-bone man who'd overheard their conversation. The book changed hands. Meanwhile, back at Pinocchio's house, poor Geppetto was shivering with cold because of that very copybook.

CHAPTER 10

When Pinocchio walked into the puppet theatre, his appearance almost started a riot. By this time the curtain was up and the performance had begun. On stage, Harlequin and Punchinello were quarrelling – as usual – and threatening to come to blows at any moment.

The audience was roaring with laughter: the puppets' bickering and name-calling was so lifelike, you'd have thought they were real people.

All of a sudden, Harlequin stopped acting. Turning to the crowd, he pointed towards someone at the back.

"Bless my soul!" he cried out. "Am I dreaming? Can that really be Pinocchio?"

"It is! It's him!" Punchinello shouted.

"It's Pinocchio!" squealed Miss Rosy, from behind the backdrop.

"Pinocchio! Pinocchio!" all the puppets began yelling. They flocked onto the stage. "Pinocchio! Our brother! Three cheers for Pinocchio!"

"Come up here, Pinocchio," called Harlequin. "Come and embrace your wooden brothers!"

Pinocchio responded to this invitation by leaping from the back of the stalls into the front row, then onto the conductor's head and finally the stage itself, where you wouldn't believe the number of hugs, kisses and friendly cuffs around the head he received from the wooden artistes.

Nobody could have denied that this was all very touching, but after a while the audience began to get impatient.

"What about the show?" voices yelled. "Get on with it!"

They were wasting their breath: the puppets' celebrations only got rowdier. Instead of returning to the script, the troupe lifted Pinocchio onto their shoulders and carried him in triumph to the footlights at the front of the stage.

At this point the puppet-master appeared. He was hulk of a man, whose looks alone were enough to scare the living daylights out of you. His beard was as black as ink and reached all the way down to the floor, so he trod on it every time he took a step. His mouth was as wide as an oven. His eyes burned like two red lanterns. He came onto the stage cracking a great whip made from plaited snakeskin and foxes' tails. At his unexpected appearance, a deadly hush fell over the whole theatre. You could have heard a midge sneeze. All the puppets – male and female – quivered like jelly.

"WHAT'S GOING ON HERE? ARE YOU TRYING TO RUIN MY SHOW?" the puppet-master bellowed at Pinocchio, in a voice so hollow he sounded like an ogre with a sore throat.

"It wasn't my fault, sir, honestly it wasn't!" Pinocchio squealed.

"Enough! I'll deal with you this evening," the huge man growled ominously.

After the end of the performance, the puppet-master went into his kitchen to check on a whole sheep he'd left roasting on the spit for his dinner. There wasn't quite enough wood to finish off the cooking, so he called Harlequin and Punchinello to him.

"There's a puppet hanging on a hook next door," he said. "Bring him to me. He looked nice and dry – he's just what I need to build up the fire."

Harlequin and Punchinello hesitated for a moment, but their master glowered at them so fiercely that they were terrified into obeying. They came back carrying Pinocchio, who was thrashing about like an eel and screaming, "Save me, Father, save me! I don't want to die!"

chapter 11

Fire-Eater (that was the puppet-master's name) may have looked frightening, with that long black beard that covered the whole of his chest and legs like an apron, but deep down he wasn't a bad man. When Pinocchio was dragged before him, struggling wildly and wailing "I don't want to die!", the big man began to feel sorry for him. He resisted for as long as he could, but finally he couldn't stop himself from letting out a resounding sneeze.

When he heard this, Harlequin, who had been standing forlornly by, drooping like a weeping willow, cheered up instantly.

"Good news, brother!" he whispered to Pinocchio. "The master has sneezed. That means he's having second thoughts. You're saved."

While most people, when they feel sorry for someone, either cry openly or at least wipe away a tear, Fire-Eater, at such moments, invariably sneezed – a way, like any other, of showing one's emotions.

"Stop snivelling!" he yelled, trying to keep up his gruff manner. "Your whining is making my nose itch... I think I'm about to ... hang on a minute ... atchoo!" He sneezed again.

"Bless you," Pinocchio said.

"Thank you," replied Fire-Eater. "Do you have a mother and father?"

"A father," Pinocchio answered. "I never knew my mother."

"How sad the poor man would be, if I had you thrown onto those burning coals," the puppet-master sighed. "Poor fellow...!" He sneezed again three times: "Atchoo ... atchoo ... atchoo..."

"Bless you," Pinocchio said again.

"Thank you," replied Fire-Eater. "Actually, I'm to be pitied too," he went on, "because, as you can see, the fire has died down and I don't have enough wood to finish cooking my roast. You'd certainly come in very handy... Oh well, never mind. I've started feeling sorry for you now, so it's too late. I'll just have to burn one of my own puppets... Constables!" he barked, and suddenly two tall, spindly wooden policemen came into the room, wearing helmets and carrying swords.

"Tie up Harlequin," Fire-Eater ordered in his hoarse voice, "and throw him on the fire. I like my mutton well done."

Imagine how Harlequin felt about this! He was so frightened, his legs gave way beneath him, and he collapsed onto the floor. When he saw this, Pinocchio threw himself at the puppet-master's feet, drenching his long beard with tears.

"Be merciful, Sir," he pleaded.

"I can't see any Sirs in this room," the puppet-master replied coldly.

"Be merciful, Your Honour!"

"I can't see any Honours in this room."

"Be merciful, Your Excellency."

Upon hearing himself being addressed as Your Excellency, Fire-Eater suddenly turned pink with pleasure and became more amenable.

"Well, what is it?" he asked Pinocchio.

"Please spare my poor friend Harlequin!"

"Absolutely not. If I'm going to spare you, he has to go on the fire: I like my meat well done."

"In that case," Pinocchio cried proudly, getting to his feet and sweeping off his bread-hat, "in that case, I know my duty. Come, Mr Policemen, tie me up and throw me onto the flames. I cannot allow my true friend Harlequin to die in my place!"

These words, spoken in a loud, heroic voice, had every puppet in the room in tears. Even the policemen were crying like babies, in spite of being made of wood.

At first Fire-Eater remained as cold and inflexible as a block of ice, but then, little by little, he began to sneeze. After four or five atchoos, he opened his arms wide.

"You're a good lad, Pinocchio," he said affectionately. "Come here and give old Fire-Eater a kiss."

Pinocchio ran over to the puppet-master, scampered like a squirrel up his long black beard and planted a big kiss on the end of his nose.

"Am I pardoned, then?" Harlequin asked, barely audible.

"You are," Fire-Eater confirmed, adding with a sigh and a shake of the head, "Never mind. This evening I'll just have to put up with medium rare mutton. But next time you'd all better watch out!"

When the news of the pardon spread, all the puppets ran onto the stage, switched on all the spotlights as if for a gala performance, and began to leap and dance around.

They were still dancing when the sun came up.

CHAPTER 12

The following day, Fire-Eater took Pinocchio to one side. "What is your father's name?" he asked him.

"Geppetto," replied the puppet.

"What is his profession?"

"Pauper."

"Does he earn much?"

"Just enough never to have a penny in his pocket. When he wanted to buy me a copybook for school, he had to sell his only jacket. It was a threadbare old thing."

"The poor devil!" exclaimed the puppet-master. "I very nearly feel sorry for him. Here, take these five gold coins. Go back and give them to your father at once, with my best wishes."

Pinocchio was thrilled, as you'd expect. He thanked the puppet-master a thousand times. After that, he hugged all the puppets in the company, one by one – even the policemen – then set off for home, beside himself with joy.

He'd gone less than half a mile when he met a fox, who had a limp in one leg, and a cat, who was blind in both eyes. They were helping each other along, as companions in misfortune should. The fox was leaning on the cat, and the cat was letting the fox lead the way.

"Good morning, Pinocchio," said the fox, bowing politely.

"How do you know my name?" asked the puppet.

"I know your father well," replied the fox.

"When did you see him last?"

"Yesterday. He was standing at his front door."

"What was he doing?"

"He was in his shirtsleeves, shivering with cold."

"Poor Father! Thank God he'll never be cold again."

"Why's that?"

"Because I'm a gentleman now – I'm rich."

"You?" scoffed the fox. "Rich?" He gave a coarse laugh. The cat sniggered, then covered it up by pretending to wash his whiskers.

"Don't laugh at me!" Pinocchio shouted angrily. He fished in his pocket for the money that Fire-Eater had given him. "I hate to show off," he said, pulling it out, "but here's the proof – five beautiful gold coins."

At the cheerful clink of money, the fox's shrivelled paw straightened for a moment. The cat's eyes opened and glowed like green lanterns, then closed again so quickly that Pinocchio noticed nothing.

"And what do you plan to do with those coins, young man?" the fox asked.

"The very first thing I'm going to do is buy my father a wonderful jacket of gold and silver cloth, with jewels for buttons. Then I'm going to buy myself a copybook."

"A copybook?"

"That's right. I'm going to go to school and start working hard."

"Oh!" the fox exclaimed. "Do be careful! Look at me. A reckless passion for swotting cost me a leg."

"And look at me: swotting cost me my sight," added the cat.

At that moment, a white blackbird who was perched on the hedge by the side of the road gave a short burst of song, then began to speak.

"Beware of false friends, Pinocchio," he warned.

The poor bird would have done better to keep his beak shut. Before he'd even had time to squawk "Help!", the cat had leapt on him and gobbled him up, feathers and all. Then he cleaned his whiskers, closed his eyes again and went back to being blind.

"Poor blackbird!" exclaimed Pinocchio. "Why did you do that?"

"To teach him a lesson," the cat replied. "Next time he'll think twice before butting in on other people's conversations."

They were almost halfway home, when the fox suddenly stopped walking and said to the puppet, "Would you like to double your money?"

"What do you mean?" asked Pinocchio.

"Would you like your five gold coins to turn into a hundred, or a thousand, or two thousand?"

"Who wouldn't! But how?"

"It's easy. But instead of going home, you'd have to come with us."

"Where to?"

"To Silly Gooseland."

Pinocchio thought for a moment, then replied firmly, "No thank you, I don't think so. I want to get home to see my father, and I'm almost there now. He must have been worried sick when I didn't come home last night! I've been very naughty. The cricket was right about bad boys always ending up in trouble. I've found that out the hard way – all sorts of horrid things have happened. I've been in terrible danger. Last night, in Fire-Eater's house..." The puppet shuddered. "It gives me the shivers just to think of it."

"Very well," the fox said, "if you're sure. Off you go. It's your loss."

"It's your loss!" echoed the cat.

"But think it over well before you go, Pinocchio," the fox said. "You're turning down a fortune."

"...down a fortune!" echoed the cat.

"Your five coins would have become two thousand – overnight."

"Overnight!" echoed the cat.

"But how?" Pinocchio gasped.

"Permit me to explain," said the fox. "In Silly Gooseland there is a sacred field, known as the Field of Miracles. In this field you make a small hole in the ground and plant – for example – a gold coin. Then you cover the hole with a little earth and water it with two bucketfuls of spring water. Finally, you sprinkle your planting-hole with a pinch of salt and retire to bed. During the night the gold coin sprouts, and grows, and flowers. The next morning, when you go back to the field, what do you find? A tree full of gold coins, that's what – as richly laden as an ear of corn in the month of June."

"So," Pinocchio asked, in growing wonder, "if I buried my five gold coins in that field, how many would there be in the morning?"

"That's a matter of simple arithmetic," the fox replied. "You can do it in your head. Let's say each coin produces five hundred more. Multiply that five hundred by five, and the next morning you'll be pocketing two thousand five hundred shiny new coins."

"Hooray!" yelled Pinocchio, jumping up and down with joy. "When I've picked them all, I'll keep two thousand for myself and give five hundred to the two of you."

"To us?" the fox cried out in horror, with a mortified look. "Heaven forfend!"

"...forfend!" echoed the cat.

"We have no interest in financial gain," the fox went on. "We strive only to enrich our fellow creatures."

"Creatures," agreed the cat.

What excellent people, Pinocchio thought to himself. And there and then he forgot his father, the new jacket, the copybook and all of his good intentions.

"Lead the way," he said. "I'll follow."

CHAPTER 13

They walked and walked until evening, when they arrived, exhausted, at the Red Lobster Inn.

"Let's stop for a while," the fox suggested, "for a bite to eat and a few hours' sleep. If we set off again at midnight we'll reach the Field of Miracles by dawn."

So they went inside. They sat down to dinner, but none of them had any appetite.

The cat had terrible indigestion and could only manage thirty-five mullets in tomato sauce and four helpings of tripe with Parmesan cheese – which was rather bland, so he had to call three times for extra cheese and butter.

The fox would gladly have nibbled a little something, but his doctor had put him on a strict diet, so he had to make do with a single dish of hare in sweet-and-sour sauce, garnished with plump spring chickens and pullets. After the hare, to clean his palate he forced down a mixed grill of partridges, rabbits, frogs, lizards and prunes in brandy. That was all he could manage, he said, because the mere sight of food made him feel quite ill.

The diner who ate least was Pinocchio. He ordered half a nut and a slice of bread but didn't touch either. The poor puppet couldn't stop thinking about the Field of Miracles, and was suffering prematurely from gold-coin dyspepsia.

After dinner, the fox asked the innkeeper for two rooms. "One for Mr Pinocchio here, and the other for myself and my companion," he said. "We'll have a short nap before we get back on the road. Could you be so kind as to wake us just before midnight?"

"Of course, Sir," replied the innkeeper with a sly wink.

Pinocchio fell asleep the moment his head hit the pillow. He dreamt he was in a field full of small trees whose branches were laden with gold coins that hung down in clusters and swayed in the wind, tinkling enticingly as if to say "Come and get us". But just as the puppet was about to reach out and stuff his pockets, he was woken abruptly by three loud knocks on his bedroom door.

It was the innkeeper, who had come to tell him it was midnight.

"Are my friends ready?" Pinocchio asked.

"You could say that," replied the innkeeper. "They left two hours ago."

"But why?" Pinocchio asked.

"The cat got a message that his oldest kitten is at death's door," said the innkeeper. "With chilblains."

"Did they pay for dinner?"

"Of course not!" exclaimed the innkeeper. "They're well-brought-up people. They wouldn't dream of being so rude."

A pity. I wouldn't have been a bit offended, thought Pinocchio, scratching his head. "And where did my good friends say we should meet?" he asked.

"In the Field of Miracles, at dawn tomorrow morning."

Pinocchio handed over a gold coin for the dinner, and left.

Outside, the night was pitch-black and he had to feel his way. In the fields around him, not a leaf stirred. From time to time the wings of some night bird would brush against his nose, making him jump back in fear and yell, "Who goes there?" The distant hills echoed: "Who goes there?"

As he walked on, he suddenly spotted a tiny creature clinging to a tree-trunk. It glowed feebly, like a china night-light.

"Who are you?" asked Pinocchio.

"I am the ghost of the talking cricket," the insect replied, in a voice so faint it could have come from the next world.

"What do you want with me?" the puppet asked.

I want to give you some advice," he said. "Go home. Give your father the four coins you have left. The poor man is sick with worry."

"Tomorrow," replied Pinocchio, "he's going to be rich. These four coins are going to turn into two thousand."

"Never trust people who promise to make you rich in a day, my child. They're mostly mad, or crooked. Take my advice and go home."

"I won't. I'm going on."

"It's very late..."

"I'm going on."

"It's very dark..."

"I'm going on."

"It's a dangerous road..."

"I'm going on."

"Remember that stubborn children who won't do as they're told always end up regretting it."

"Here we go again," Pinocchio groaned rudely. "The same old story. Goodnight, cricket."

"Goodnight, Pinocchio. May heaven preserve you from damp night air and assassins lurking in the shadows."

With these words, the cricket's light went out suddenly, like a snuffed candle. The road ahead looked darker than ever.

chapter 14

It's so unfair, Pinocchio thought bitterly as he set off again along the road. When you're a child, every grown-up you meet thinks they have the right to scold you and tell you what to do. They all behave like parents or teachers, every last one of them – even the crickets. And now, just because I won't do what that dreary old insect said, all kinds of calamities are supposed to descend on me. I'm even going to meet assassins, according to him. It's a good job I don't believe in assassins. I never have done. I think they were invented by parents to frighten children who want to go out alone at night. And if I did meet assassins, do you think I'd be scared? Not me. I'd go right up to them, and I'd say, "What can I do for you, my dear assassins? You'd better watch it; don't tangle with me. Buzz off and leave me alone." That would do it. And if they were rude enough not to run away ... well in that case I'd run instead, and that'd be the end of it...

Pinocchio never finished his train of thought: at that moment he heard a rustling of leaves behind him. He turned round and saw two sinister black figures tiptoeing towards him in the darkness. They were covered from head to toe in large coalsacks, and were bounding along as silently as ghosts.

It's them! he panicked. Not knowing where to hide his money, he slipped it under his tongue. Then he tried to run away, but before he could take a single step he felt himself being seized by both arms.

"Your money or your life!" said two ghastly, cavernous voices.

Pinocchio couldn't reply, because his mouth was full of gold coins, so he bowed and scraped to his two captors, whose eyes were only visible through the small holes in their hoods. He tried his best to indicate, through gestures, that he was only a poor puppet, without a penny to his name.

"Stop chattering!" they shouted menacingly. "Out with your money!"

Pinocchio shook his head. He opened his arms wide, to show that he had nothing on him.

"Hand it over, or you're dead meat!" said the taller assassin.

"Meat!" echoed his companion.

"And after we've killed you, we'll kill your father," the first one went on.

"No, no, not my poor father!" Pinocchio cried desperately. As he spoke, the coins clinked in his mouth.

"Aha! You've hidden it under your tongue, you little fiend! Spit it out this minute!" they commanded.

But Pinocchio was having none of it.

"So you've gone deaf, have you?" cried the murderers. "Then we'll just have to make you!" One of them seized Pinocchio by the nose while the other grabbed his chin. They began to tug in different directions, trying to force his mouth open. But it was no use: the puppet's wooden mouth might as well have been nailed shut.

At this point the smaller assassin produced a knife and tried to slip it between Pinocchio's lips, as a lever. Quick as a flash, the puppet sank his teeth into his tormentor's hand and bit it clean off. When he spat it out, he was amazed to find that it wasn't a hand at all, but a cat's paw.

Heartened by this small victory, Pinocchio clawed himself free from his attackers and leapt over the hedge by the side of the road. He fled across the fields with the assassins at his heels like hounds chasing a hare.

After ten miles, Pinocchio was too exhausted to take another step. Fearing for his life, he shinned up a very tall pine tree and sat himself in the highest branches. The assassins tried to follow him, but halfway up they lost their grip and slipped back to the ground, grazing themselves as they did so.

But they weren't beaten yet. They piled dry wood at the foot of the pine, then set fire to it. In next to no time the tree was burning fiercely. Pinocchio saw the flames leap higher and higher and – since he didn't want to end up like a Sunday roast – he took a huge leap down from the top of the tree and set off again, running across fields and vineyards. The assassins followed tirelessly.

As day began to break, they were all still running. Suddenly Pinocchio found his way barred by a deep, wide ditch full of water the colour of milky coffee. For a moment he was stumped. Then he counted to three, took a long run up and leapt across to the other side. The assassins jumped too, but they misjudged the distance and fell headlong into the ditch. Pinocchio heard them land in the water and then start thrashing about.

"Enjoy your swim, my dear assassins!" he shouted over his shoulder, laughing as he ran.

At last the weary puppet thought his pursuers must have drowned, but when he looked back he realized they were still on his heels, wrapped up in their sacks and dripping water like two colanders.

Chapter 15

It was at this point that Pinocchio almost lost heart. About to throw himself to the ground and give up, he noticed something pale glimmering in the distance, among the dark green of the trees. It was a little white cottage.

If I could just reach that house I might be safe, he thought.

Wasting no time, he started off again, careering through the wood with the assassins close behind.

After a desperate chase which lasted almost two hours, he arrived, gasping, at the white cottage, and knocked on the front door.

There was no reply.

He knocked again, longer and harder, because he could hear the steps of his panting tormentors drawing closer and closer.

Still there was no reply.

When he realized that knocking was not going to do any good, he began to bang his head against the door in desperation. A beautiful little girl opened the window. Her hair was deep blue. Her face was as pale as wax. Her eyes were closed, and her hands were crossed on her breast.

"Nobody is living here," she said, in an otherworldly voice and without visibly moving her lips. "Everyone is dead."

"Can you open the door for me, please?" Pinocchio pleaded, sobbing.

"I, too, am dead," the girl replied.

"Dead? Then what are you doing at the window?"

"I am waiting for the hearse to come and take me away."

With these words, the girl disappeared and the window closed quietly.

"Open the door, pretty blue-haired girl!" Pinocchio cried. "Take pity on a poor boy cruelly pursued by assass..."

Before he could finish, he felt himself being seized by the neck.

"You're not getting away this time," growled the now-familiar voices.

The puppet, who realized he was staring death in the face, began to quiver so violently that the joints in his wooden legs rattled and the coins under his tongue clinked merrily.

"Are you going to open your mouth or not?" the assassins asked. "You won't answer, eh? Never mind. We'll do it for you."

Pulling out two long, razor-sharp knives, they tried to stab him twice in the back, but luckily Pinocchio was made of very hard wood and the knives shattered into a thousand pieces. The assassins were left holding the handles and staring at each other in surprise.

"All right, then," said one of them. "We'll have to hang him."

The two villains tied Pinocchio's hands behind his back, put a noose around his neck and hanged him from a tall tree known as the Great Oak. Then they sat down on the grass, waiting for their victim to stop kicking. But after three hours, the puppet's eyes were still wide open, his mouth was still tightly shut and he was kicking away like anything. Eventually they got bored.

"See you tomorrow," they sneered. "We hope you'll be kind enough to let us find you good and dead, with your mouth wide open." And with that they left.

A strong north wind had risen. It whistled and groaned, swinging the poor puppet back and forth like the clapper of a church bell at a royal wedding. His neck hurt terribly, and the noose was growing tighter, making it harder and harder to breathe. His eyes began to grow dim. He could feel death drawing closer, yet he still hoped that somebody would come by and get him down. He waited and waited, but finally he realized that it was all in vain: nobody was going to save him. His thoughts turned to Geppetto.

"If only you were here with me, Father," he murmured. Then he had no strength left to speak. His eyes closed. His mouth fell open. His legs stretched out and, with one last shudder, he stiffened and hung there, quite still.

CHAPTER 16

As Pinocchio was hanging from the branch of the Great Oak, looking more dead than alive, the little blue-haired girl came to her window again. Overwhelmed with pity at the sight of this poor soul dancing a jig in the gusts of the north wind, she clapped her hands three times and there was a sound of flapping wings. A great hawk landed on the windowsill.

"What is your command, oh beautiful fairy?" the hawk asked, bowing his head. (The little blue-haired girl was actually a good fairy who had been living in the house by the wood for more than a thousand years.)

"Do you see that puppet hanging from a branch of the Great Oak?" the fairy asked.

"I do," replied the hawk.

"I want you to fly over there at once. Use your strong beak to cut him free, then lay him down as gently as you can on the grass at the foot of the tree," the fairy commanded.

The hawk flew off. In just two minutes, he was back.

"I have done as you asked," he said.

"Was the puppet dead or alive?" the fairy asked.

"He looked dead," replied the hawk, "but he can't have been, because when I cut the noose from his neck, he sighed and whispered, 'That's better!'"

The fairy clapped her hands twice, and a handsome poodle came into the room. He was walking on his hindlegs, like a man, and wearing a coachman's uniform. It was a splendid outfit: on his head there was a gold-trimmed, three-cornered hat. Beneath it, he wore a curly white wig which reached down to his shoulders. His jacket was chocolate-brown, with jewelled buttons and two large pockets to hold the bones his mistress gave him for lunch. He wore breeches of crimson velvet, silk stockings and smart little shoes. His tail had a blue satin cover on it, which kept it dry when it rained.

"Be a good dog, Medoro," said the fairy. "Get my best carriage from the stable and drive into the wood. When you reach the Great Oak, you'll see a half-dead puppet lying on the ground. Lift him up carefully. Make him comfortable on the cushions in the carriage and bring him back here. Is that clear?"

The poodle wagged his blue tail-cover three or four times, to show that he had understood, and hurried off as fast as he could.

Not long after, a wonderful carriage drove out of the fairy's stables. It was the colour of air, upholstered with whipped cream and biscuits, with cushions of canary feathers. In the traces were a hundred pairs of white mice. Up on the box sat the poodle, cracking his whip from side to side.

In less than quarter of an hour the carriage was back. The fairy, who had been waiting on the doorstep, lifted the puppet out herself and carried him to a bedroom with walls made of mother-of-pearl. Then she sent for the best doctors in the area. They arrived in seconds, one after the other: a crow, an owl and a cricket.

"Could you three gentlemen please tell me whether this puppet is alive or dead?" the fairy asked, as these distinguished physicians gathered around Pinocchio's bed.

The crow came forward first. He took Pinocchio's pulse. He felt his nose, then the little toe on each of his feet. When he had concluded his examination, he declared solemnly: "In my opinion the patient is dead, but if by some mischance he isn't, then that would be a sure sign that he was alive."

"It pains me to have to contradict my learned friend," the owl interrupted, "but in my opinion the patient is alive. If, however, by some mischance he isn't, then that would be a sure sign that he was dead."

"What about you?" the fairy asked the cricket. "Do you have nothing to say?"

"In my opinion," replied the cricket, "when a prudent doctor doesn't know what he is talking about, he holds his tongue. In any case, this puppet is no stranger to me; I've known him for some time."

Pinocchio – who had, until then, been lying as still as a common-or-garden block of wood – suddenly quivered so violently that the whole bed shook.

"This patient," the cricket went on, "is the naughtiest ..." – Pinocchio opened his eyes, then shut them again – "rudest, laziest, most disobedient ..." – the puppet hid his head under the sheets – "stubborn child I have ever met. He is making his old father sick with worry."

And then the room was filled with the sound of muffled sobs. Imagine everyone's surprise when they peered beneath the sheets and saw that the sound was coming from Pinocchio.

"When a dead man weeps," the crow said solemnly, "it is a sure sign that he is on the mend."

"It pains me to have to contradict my learned friend and colleague," interrupted the owl, "but in my opinion, when a dead man weeps it is a sure sign that he is not entirely happy to be dead."

CHAPTER 17

As soon as the three doctors had left the room, the fairy went over to Pinocchio, felt his forehead and realized that he had a high fever.

She poured some white powder into half a glass of water, stirred it and handed it to him.

"Drink this," she said gently. "You'll feel better in a few days' time."

Pinocchio looked at the glass. He pulled a face.

"Is it sweet," he asked doubtfully, "or bitter?"

"It's bitter, but it'll do you good," the fairy replied.

"If it's bitter, I won't drink it."

"It'll help you get better..."

"I can't stand bitter drinks."

"If you drink it, I'll give you some sugar to take the taste away."

"Where's the sugar?"

"Here," said the fairy, taking a sugar-lump from a golden bowl.

"Give me the sugar first," said Pinocchio, "and I'll drink that nasty water afterwards."

"Do you promise to drink it?"

"Yes."

The fairy handed over the sugar-lump. Pinocchio crunched it up and swallowed it in a flash.

"Wouldn't it be great if sugar was a medicine!" he exclaimed, licking his lips. "I'd take a large dose every day."

"Now keep your promise and drink these few drops of medicine," said the fairy. "They'll make you better."

Pinocchio took the glass reluctantly. He stuck his nose in it and sniffed. He brought it to his mouth, then hesitated. He stuck his nose in it again.

"It's too bitter," he said at last. "I can't drink it."

"How do you know it's bitter, if you haven't even tasted it?"

"I can tell. It smells bitter. I want another sugar-lump, then I'll drink it."

With a mother's patience, the fairy placed another sugar-lump on his tongue, then presented him with the glass for a second time.

"I can't drink it like this!" the puppet whined, pulling a face.

"What do you mean?"

"I'm not comfortable. It's that pillow on my feet. It's bothering me."

The fairy took the pillow away.

"I still can't drink it."

"What is it now?"

"The bedroom door's half open."

The fairy shut the door.

"Oh anyway," Pinocchio yelled, bursting into tears. "I shan't drink this horrid water. I shan't, I shan't, I shan't!"

"You'll be sorry, my child."

"Don't care."

"This fever could kill you in just a few hours."

"Don't care."

"You're not afraid of dying?"

"Not in the least. I'd rather die than drink that rotten medicine."

At these words, the bedroom door flew open. In came four rabbits, as black as ink, carrying a small coffin on their shoulders.

"What do you want?" cried Pinocchio, sitting bolt upright in terror.

"To take you away," replied the largest rabbit.

"Take me away? But I'm not dead yet."

"Not yet, but since you've refused to take the medicine, you've only a few minutes left."

"Fairy!" Pinocchio squealed. "Pass me the medicine! Quick! I don't want to die! I don't want to die!"

He took the glass and gulped the contents down in one go.

"A wasted journey," sighed the rabbits. "Never mind." And they hoisted the coffin back onto their shoulders and left the room, grumbling quietly to themselves.

After just a few minutes Pinocchio jumped down from his bed, quite well again. Wooden puppets, you see, are lucky: they very seldom fall ill, and when they do they get better very quickly.

At the sight of Pinocchio prancing round the room, the fairy said, "So my medicine worked then?"

"It certainly did!" cried Pinocchio. "I feel like a new puppet!"

"So why did you make such a fuss about drinking it?" the fairy asked.

"That's children for you – we're more afraid of the medicine than the disease," replied Pinocchio.

"Well, that's very silly, because the right medicine, taken in time, can save your life."

"Don't worry, I won't be so difficult next time. I'll remember the black rabbits and take my medicine straight away."

"Now," said the fairy, "sit next to me and tell me how you came to be chased by those villains."

"Well," Pinocchio began, "what happened was that Fire-Eater the puppet-master gave me some gold coins and told me to take them to my father, but along the way I met this wonderful couple – a fox and a cat – and they asked would I like the coins to turn into a thousand, or two thousand, and said that if I went with them to the Field of Miracles, they'd show me how. So I said, 'Yes', and they said, 'Let's stop at this inn, and we'll be off again at midnight,' but when I woke up they'd already left, so I set off on my own, but it was pitch-black, and I met these two assassins with coal sacks over their heads. They said, 'Your money or your life,' and I said I didn't have any money – 'cos I'd hidden it under my tongue, you see. Then one of them tried to put his hand in my mouth, and I bit it off, but it wasn't a hand – it was a paw. And the assassins kept chasing me, and I ran until they caught up with me and hanged me from a tree in the wood over there, so that when they got back I'd be dead, with my mouth wide open, and they'd get the money from under my tongue."

"So where are the four coins now?" the fairy asked.

"I lost them," lied Pinocchio (who had them in his pocket).

No sooner had this lie passed his lips than his nose – which was already long – grew a whole five centimetres.

"Where did you lose them?" the fairy asked.

"In the wood," replied the puppet. His nose grew still longer.

"If you lost them there, we'll go and look for them," she said. "Everything that is lost in that wood is always found again."

"Ah," Pinocchio said quickly. "Now I remember. I didn't lose them, I swallowed them by mistake while I was taking my medicine."

This third fib made his nose grow so ridiculously long that poor Pinocchio was completely stuck. If he turned to the left, his nose bumped into the bed or the window. If he turned the other way, it was trapped by the wall or the bedroom door. When he tried lifting his head a little, he almost poked the good fairy in the eye.

The fairy was looking at him, laughing.

"What are you laughing at?" Pinocchio asked, confused.

"Your lie," she replied.

"But how do you know I lied?"

"Lies are easy to recognize, my child. There are two kinds: lies with short legs and lies with long noses. Your lie is of the long-nosed variety."

Pinocchio wanted to hide away in shame, but when he tried to run out of the room, he couldn't. His nose had grown so long it wouldn't fit through the door.

CHAPTER 18

It may not surprise you to learn that the good fairy – seeking to cure Pinocchio of the nasty habit of telling lies – left him to scream and wail for a good half-hour. But when she saw that he had worked himself up into such a state that his eyes were bulging out of his head, she relented and clapped her hands. At this summons thousands of woodpeckers flew in through the window. They perched on Pinocchio's preposterous nose and began to peck away at it so vigorously that in just a few minutes it was back to its normal size.

"Thank you, dear fairy!" said Pinocchio, drying his eyes. "You're so good to me, and I love you so much."

"I love you too," the fairy replied. "If you'd like to stay here with me, we could live together like brother and sister."

"Yes, please!" cried Pinocchio. "But what about my father?"

"I've arranged everything. I sent him a message, and he'll be here before nightfall."

"Really?" cried Pinocchio, jumping for joy. "In that case, would you mind if I went to meet him on the road? I can't wait to give him a great big hug – I've made his life such a misery. Poor Father."

"Of course you may, but do be careful not to get lost. Stick to the path through the wood, and you'll be sure to meet him."

Pinocchio set off. As soon as he got among the trees he began to run like the wind. When he drew level with the Great Oak, he stopped, because he thought he could hear a rustling in the undergrowth. And sure enough, out of the bushes popped his old travelling companions, the fox and the cat.

"My dear Pinocchio!" cried the fox, kissing the puppet on both cheeks. "What brings you to these parts?"

"These parts?" echoed the cat.

"It's a long story," replied the puppet. "I'll tell you properly when I have more time. But, the other night, when you left me at the inn, I met these assassins on the road..."

"Assassins?" cried the fox in horror. "Oh, my poor friend! What did they want?"

"My money."

"The villains!" exclaimed the fox.

"Villains!" echoed the cat.

"I tried to escape," the puppet said, "but they caught up with me. Then they hanged me from that tree over there –" he pointed to the Great Oak.

"What a dreadful story," the fox sighed. "I don't know what the world is coming to. What are we decent folk supposed to do?"

As they stood there talking, Pinocchio noticed that the cat's front right-hand paw was missing, claws and all.

"What happened to your paw?" he asked.

The cat began to mumble something but the fox interrupted.

"My wounded friend is too modest," he said. "Allow me to tell you. No more than an hour ago, on this very road, we met a poor, flea-bitten old wolf, who was weak with hunger. He begged us for something to eat, but we didn't have so much as a fish bone between us. So can you guess what my tender-hearted friend did...? He bit off one of his front paws, and threw it to the poor creature for his lunch."

The fox wiped away a tear as he spoke. Pinocchio, too, was deeply moved.

"If only there were more cats like you around!" he whispered in the cat's ear. "Mice would finally live in peace."

"So what are you up to now?" the fox asked the puppet.

"I'm waiting for my father. He should be here at any moment."

"And your gold coins?"

"They're still in my pocket, except for the one I spent at the inn."

"And to think that instead of four you could have had a thousand," the fox sighed, "or even two! Why don't you take my advice and go to the Field of Miracles to bury them?"

"I can't," Pinocchio replied, "not today. I'll go another day."

"Another day will be too late," said the fox.

"Why?"

"Because the field has been bought by a rich man, and he isn't going to allow anybody to bury coins any more, as of tomorrow."

"How far is this Field of Miracles?" Pinocchio asked.

"Just a couple of miles. Why don't you come with us? We'll be there in half an hour. You can bury your coins the moment you get there. Before you know it you'll have two thousand more, and by this evening you'll be back home, your pockets bulging with gold."

Pinocchio hesitated. He thought of the good fairy. He thought of Geppetto, and the cricket's dire warnings. Then he did what you'd expect of a heartless child without an ounce of common sense – he shrugged his shoulders and said, "Lead the way. I'll follow."

And off they went.

After half a day's walk, they reached a place named Swindleton. Pinocchio noticed that the streets were full of miserable creatures. There were mangy dogs yawning with hunger, and shorn sheep trembling with cold. There were crestless chickens begging for corn, and large butterflies who'd sold their wings and could no longer fly. There were shamefaced peacocks trying to hide their plucked behinds, and depressed pheasants who wandered about dreaming of the bright gold-and-silver feathers they had lost for ever.

Every now and then a grand carriage would make its way through this tattered menagerie, usually carrying a fox, a magpie or a carrion-bird.

"Where is the Field of Miracles?" Pinocchio asked.

"Just around the corner," replied the fox.

They crossed to the other side of town. Once they were beyond the city walls, they stopped in a lonely field that looked no different from those around it.

"Here we are," the fox said to the puppet. "Now, dig a little planting-hole with your hands and put in the coins."

Pinocchio followed the fox's instructions. He dug the hole, put his four remaining coins into the bottom and covered them with soil. "Now go to the stream at the bottom of the hill," said the fox, "fill a bucket, and use it to water your planting-hole."

Pinocchio went down to the stream. Since he didn't have a bucket, he took off a shoe, filled it and watered the soil with that.

"Is there anything else I need to do?" he asked.

"Nothing," replied the fox. "We can all leave now. You come back here in twenty minutes or so and you'll find a bush has sprouted, with its branches already full of coins."

The puppet was overjoyed. He thanked his companions again and again, promising them a generous reward.

"We don't want money," said the two ruffians. "It is enough to have shown you the simple art of getting rich quickly."

With these words, they bade Pinocchio farewell, wished him an excellent harvest and went on their way.

Chapter 19

The puppet walked back into town, counting the minutes one by one. When he felt he'd waited long enough, he headed back to the Field of Miracles. As he rushed along, his racing heart was going tick-tock, tick-tock, like an over-wound grandfather clock.

What if I found not one thousand coins, but two? he thought to himself. Or instead of two thousand, five? Or instead of five, a hundred? A hundred thousand coins! I'd have a beautiful villa and a thousand wooden horses with a thousand toy stables to keep them in. I'd have a cellar full of fruit cordials and wines and a library crammed with sweets, candied fruit, cakes, biscuits, cream buns...

Daydreaming in this fashion, he soon came within sight of the Field of Miracles. He stopped, hoping to spot a sapling laden with gold, but he saw nothing. He walked on a bit further: nothing. He went right into the field and up to the place where he'd buried his coins: still nothing.

Forgetting his manners, he pulled his hand out of his pocket to give his head a good long scratch. Just then a raucous laugh rang in his ears. Looking up he saw a large parrot, perched on a branch, preening his few remaining feathers.

"What are you laughing at?" snapped Pinocchio.

"I tickled myself while I was preening under my wing," replied the bird.

The puppet made no comment. He went to the stream, filled his shoe again and gave his coins another watering. A second laugh broke the silence. It was even more insolent than the first. Pinocchio lost his temper.

"Tell me what you're laughing about, you rude bird!" he shouted.

"I'm laughing about those silly geese who believe all they hear and get cheated by people with more brains than them," came the reply.

"Do you mean me?"

"I do, poor Pinocchio, I do. I'm laughing at you, and the idea that money can be planted and harvested like beans or pumpkins. I believed it too, once upon a time, and look at what it did to me. Now I've learned – too late – that if you want money, you have to earn it honestly, either with your muscles or your brain."

"I don't understand," said the puppet, although he was starting to tremble as the truth dawned on him.

"I'll do my best to speak plainly," said the parrot. "While you were away in town, the fox and the cat came back. They dug up your money and ran off with it. They'll be miles away by now."

Pinocchio's jaw dropped. Not wanting to believe the parrot's words, he began to scrabble in the freshly-watered earth. He dug and dug until the hole he'd made was so large you could have buried a haystack in it, but the money was nowhere to be seen.

Desperate, he ran back into town and went straight to the court-house, to press charges against the two thieves.

The judge was a venerable old monkey, with a venerable white beard and a very venerable pair of gold-rimmed spectacles, with no lenses, which he was forced to wear on account of an infection that had been troubling him for years.

When Pinocchio came before the judge, he explained the despicable trick that had been played on him. He gave the names and descriptions of the two villains and ended by asking for justice.

The venerable monkey listened with interest. He nodded sympathetically, and even wiped away a tear. Then, when the story was over, he reached out and rang a bell.

Two mastiffs in constable's uniforms came into the courtroom.

"This poor devil has had four gold coins stolen from him," the judge said to them. "Take him to the cells."

When Pinocchio heard this, he was dumbfounded. He was about to protest, but the policemen avoided any pointless time-wasting by covering his mouth and dragging him off to jail.

Which was where he remained for four whole months. It would have been longer, except that he had a stroke of luck: the young emperor who ruled over Swindleton, having won a great victory against his enemy, ordered public celebrations, including illuminations, fireworks, races and, as a final grand gesture, freedom for all the villains in the city's prisons.

"If they're being let out, I should be too," Pinocchio said to his jailer.

"No, not you," the man replied. "You're not a villain."

"I am, I really am," insisted Pinocchio. "I'm an incorrigible scoundrel."

"I do beg your pardon," said the jailer. "My mistake."

He opened the door of Pinocchio's cell, doffed his cap and bade him a polite farewell.

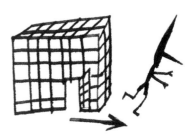

CHAPTER 20

As Pinocchio walked free he was jubilant and wasted no time getting out of the city and onto the road to the good fairy's house.

It was raining and the road was knee-deep in mud, but Pinocchio barely noticed: he was so eager to see his father and his pretty blue-haired sister that he bounded along like a greyhound, splattering himself in mud from head to foot.

What a terrible time I've had! he said to himself as he ran. But I deserved it all. I'm stubborn and touchy. I always want to do just as I like. I won't listen to people who love me and have a lot more sense than I do. But I'm going to change. I'm going to be good and do as I'm told. Disobedience never brings you anything but trouble.

Will my father be waiting for me? I wonder if he's still at the fairy's house. I haven't seen him for so long; I can't wait to throw my arms around him. I do hope the fairy will forgive me... When I think how kind she was, and how well she looked after me! I owe her my life. How could I have been so selfish and ungrateful?

All of a sudden, Pinocchio stopped in his tracks, then staggered back in fear.

Lying across his path was a huge snake. It was green, with eyes like burning coals and a pointed tail that smoked like a chimney.

The puppet was so terrified that he ran half a mile back down the road and sat on a pile of stones, to wait until the reptile moved on and left the coast clear.

An hour went by, then two, then three, but the snake didn't budge. Even from his safe distance, Pinocchio could see the glow of its fiery eyes and the column of smoke rising from the tip of its tail. In the end he plucked up the courage to approach it.

"Pardon me, Mr Snake," he said in as small and ingratiating a voice as he could muster. "Could you possibly be so good as to move over just a teeny little bit, so I can get through?"

He might as well have been talking to a brick wall.

"You see, Mr Snake," he went on in the same little voice, "I'm on my way home, and my father's waiting for me, and I haven't seen him for such a long time! Would you very much mind letting me carry on with my journey?"

He waited for some reply, but none came – in fact the snake, which up until then had looked perfectly well, began to move less and less, until it appeared to stiffen. Finally its eyes closed and its tail stopped smoking.

I think I may be in luck, Pinocchio thought, rubbing his hands together with delight. I think it may be dead.

Eager to get on, he went to step over the snake's body. He hadn't even finished lifting his foot when the snake sprang up like a Jack-in-the-box. Pinocchio drew back in fear, tripped, and fell so awkwardly that he ended up with his head in the mud and his legs waving about in the air.

At the sight of the puppet's legs pedalling frantically in mid-air, the snake began to laugh. It carried on laughing so long and so hard that it burst a blood vessel in its heart and fell to the ground. This time it really was dead.

Pinocchio started to run again as fast as he could, so as to reach the fairy's house before nightfall. But he was famished, and soon he couldn't resist sneaking into a vineyard to pick a few bunches of muscatel grapes.

This, however, turned out to have been a bad idea. When the puppet went up to one of the vines he heard something go crack! and felt his legs being crushed between two sharp bits of iron that hurt so much he saw stars.

Pinocchio had been caught in a trap, set by local farmers to catch some large polecats that had been terrorizing every henhouse in the neighbourhood.

Chapter 21

Pinocchio began to sob and yell for help, but it was no good. There were no houses near by and the road was deserted.

Night fell. Pinocchio, who was in agony from the pain in his shins and very afraid of being all alone in the fields at night, felt that he was about to faint away. All of a sudden he saw a firefly flit past his head.

"Little firefly!" he called out. "Please, please can you help me out of this mess?"

"Poor child!" the firefly exclaimed in horror. "How on earth did you get stuck in those metal jaws?"

"I wanted to pick grapes, and—"

"Were the grapes yours?"

"I was hungry..."

"Hunger is no excuse for stealing, my boy."

"You're right!" Pinocchio wailed, "You're right! I won't do it again."

They were interrupted by the muffled sound of footsteps. It was the owner of the vineyard, tiptoeing over to check his trap. Imagine his amazement when, pulling a lantern from beneath his coat, he discovered not the polecat that had been eating his chickens, but a wooden boy.

"So you're the one who's been stealing my hens!" he bellowed. "You little thief!"

"No!" sobbed Pinocchio. "I only came here to pick a few grapes..."

"People who steal grapes are quite capable of stealing chickens too," said the farmer. "I'll teach you a lesson you won't forget in a hurry." And he opened the trap, picked up the puppet by the scruff of the neck and carried him home under his arm, like a newborn lamb.

When they reached the farm, the man threw Pinocchio to the ground and put a foot on his neck.

"It's late now," he said, "and I want to go to bed. I'll deal with you in the morning.

In the meantime, since my guard dog died today, you can take his place and keep an eye on the farm for me."

He fastened a broad studded dog-collar around Pinocchio's neck, and tightened it so the puppet couldn't slip his head out. A long metal chain connected the collar to the wall of the house.

"If it rains, you can use that kennel over there. It's still got the straw my poor old dog slept on for four years," said the farmer.

"Oh yes – and if you see any thieves, be sure to prick up your ears and bark." Then he went into the house, bolting the door behind him.

Poor Pinocchio was left alone, sitting on the ground in the yard, worn out with cold, hunger and fear. From time to time he tugged miserably at the collar round his neck, crying and talking to himself.

"I deserve this," he said. "I wish I didn't, but I do. I chose to be lazy; I chose to get into bad company, and this is where it's got me. If only I'd behaved, like other children. If only I'd gone to school and worked hard. If only I hadn't run away from my poor old father. I wouldn't be out here in the middle of nowhere, guarding a farm. If only I could start all over again! But it's too late now. I'll just have to put up with it."

And with that, he crawled into the kennel and fell asleep.

Chapter 22

Pinocchio had been sound asleep for more than two hours when he was woken, towards midnight, by strange little voices whispering outside his kennel. Poking his nose out, he saw four dark-furred animals conferring in the middle of the farmyard. They looked rather like cats, but they weren't: they were polecats – animals that are particularly fond of eggs and plump young hens. One of these polecats left the group and went over to the kennel.

"Good evening, Melampo," he said.

"My name isn't Melampo," replied Pinocchio.

"Who are you then?"

"Pinocchio."

"What are you doing here?"

"Guarding the farm."

"But where's Melampo – the old dog who used to live in this kennel?"

"He died this morning."

"He's dead? Poor Melampo! Such a kind soul! But from the look of you, I'd say you're a good dog too."

"I beg your pardon, but I'm not a dog."

"What are you then?"

"I'm a puppet."

"A puppet guarding a farm?"

"I'm afraid so. I'm being punished."

"Well," said the polecat, "let me tell you about the arrangement we had with Melampo. I'm sure you'll like it."

"What is it?" asked Pinocchio.

"One night a week we visit the henhouse and take away eight hens. We eat seven of them and leave one for you – on condition that you pretend to sleep and never, ever wake the farmer by barking."

"Is that really what Melampo used to do?" Pinocchio asked.

"It is. We always got on well," replied the polecat. "So, you go back to bed, have a nice long sleep, and when you wake up you'll find a chicken on top of the kennel, ready for your breakfast. Is that clear?"

"Perfectly," Pinocchio replied, but there was a hint of menace in his voice which implied "Just you wait till later".

The four intruders, however, thought they were safe, and made straight for the henhouse. Using their teeth and claws, they prized its small wooden door open and slipped in one after the other. But as the last one crossed the threshold, they heard the door slam shut behind them.

Pinocchio, having trapped the thieves, thought it best to be safe and rolled a large stone against the door as well. Then he began to bark, just like a guard dog.

When the farmer heard the commotion, he jumped out of bed, seized his gun and leant out of his bedroom window.

"What is it?" he called down.

"Burglars!" replied the puppet.

"Where?"

"In the henhouse."

"I'll be right down," said the farmer, and he was in the yard in the twinkling of an eye. He ran into the henhouse, caught the polecats and bundled them up in a big sack.

"Got you at last, you scoundrels!" he cried. "I'd have every right to punish you, but I'm too kind-hearted. I'll just take you to the innkeeper in the village. He'll cook you and put you on the menu as jugged hare."

Then the farmer went over to Pinocchio and patted his head.

"How did you manage to unmask their plot, when Melampo never noticed anything?" he asked.

At this point the puppet could have told him about the arrangement

between the guard dog and the polecats, but he thought, Why speak ill of the dead? They're best left in peace.

"So tell me," the farmer insisted. "Were you awake when they came?"

"I was asleep," replied Pinocchio, "but they woke me with their whispering, and then offered to give me a chicken if I promised not to bark and wake you. The cheek of it! I may be far from perfect, but I'd never cover up for criminals."

"Good for you, my boy!" the farmer cried, slapping Pinocchio on the back. "Such sentiments do you credit. And just to show how pleased I am, I'm going to let you go." And he took the dog-collar off Pinocchio's neck.

chapter 23

As soon as the humiliating weight of the dog-collar was lifted from around Pinocchio's neck, he fled through the fields and didn't stop until he reached the road to the good fairy's house.

In the valley below he could make out the wood where he'd met the fox and the cat; he could also see, high above the other trees, the top of the Great Oak, where they'd hanged him. But no matter how hard he looked, the pretty little girl's cottage was nowhere to be seen.

He was suddenly overcome by a deep sense of foreboding, and he started to run again, as fast as his tired legs could carry him. Soon he was standing in the meadow where the white cottage used to be. It had completely disappeared, and in its place was a small marble headstone, on which was carved this inscription:

IN *memory* OF
THE LITTLE BLUE-Haired GIRL
WHO DIED OF SORROW
at BEING ABANDONED
by HER BROTHER, PINOCCHIO

I'll leave you to imagine how Pinocchio felt once he'd deciphered these words. He fell to the ground and burst into floods of tears, kissing the headstone over and over again. He lay there all night long, and when dawn broke he was still sobbing, even though his eyes had run out of tears. His cries were so loud and piercing that they echoed from the surrounding hills.

"Why did you have to die?" he wailed. "You were so good and I'm so bad. Why couldn't I have died instead? And what has become of my father? Tell me, my beloved fairy, and I'll never, ever leave him again."

"It can't be true that you're dead!" he went on. "If you really loved your little brother, you'd come back to life. Don't you feel sorry for me, all alone with no one to look after me? If those murderers came back now they'd hang me again, and this time I'd die for ever. How am I going to survive, all by myself in this big wide world? Who's going to feed me, now that I've lost you and my father? Where will I sleep? Who will buy me clothes? I'd be better off dead too. I want to die..." He tried to tear his hair out but, since it was made of wood, he couldn't even get his fingers into it.

As he lay on the ground weeping, he caught the attention of a large dove flying overhead.

"What are you doing, child?" the bird called out, hovering above Pinocchio.

"Can't you see I'm crying?" the puppet replied, lifting his face towards the voice and drying his eyes on his sleeve.

"Tell me," the dove went on, "do you by any chance know a puppet called Pinocchio? Is he one of your schoolmates, perhaps?"

"Did you say Pinocchio?" cried the puppet, jumping up. "That's me!"

97

The dove flew down. Once it was on the ground next to him, Pinocchio could see that it was larger than a turkey.

"In that case, you must know Geppetto," it said.

"Know him?" said Pinocchio. "He's my father! Has he spoken about me? Is he alive? Please, please tell me - is he alive?"

"I saw him three days ago, on the edge of the sea."

"What was he doing there?"

"He was building himself a small boat. The poor man has been searching for you all over the world for more than four months. Now, because he couldn't find you anywhere, he's got it into his head to go and look on the other side of the ocean, in the New World."

"How far is it to the sea?" Pinocchio asked urgently.

"More than a thousand miles," the dove replied.

"A thousand miles?" Pinocchio cried. "Oh, I wish I had wings like you!"

"I can take you there if you want," the bird offered.

"How?"

"On my back. Do you weigh much?"

"I'm as light as a feather!" cried Pinocchio. He clambered onto the dove's back, sitting astride him like a man riding a horse. "Let's go!" he yelled happily. "I can't wait to see him!"

The dove took to the air, and soon they were so high up that they almost touched the clouds. The puppet looked down out of curiosity, but he was seized by such vertigo that he had to fling his arms around the neck of his feathered steed and cling on for dear life.

They flew all day. When evening fell, the dove said he was thirsty.

"And I'm starving," Pinocchio added.

"Let's have a rest at that dovecote down there," the bird suggested.

"Then we'll set off again, and reach the sea tomorrow morning."

The dovecote was deserted. There was nothing there but a bucket of water and a basket full of a plant called hairy vetch.

Pinocchio had never been able to eat that kind of thing – he said hairy leaves tickled his throat and made him feel sick – but that evening he ate and ate. When the basket was almost empty he turned to the dove and exclaimed, "I'd never have believed that vetch could be so tasty!"

"It just goes to show that you'll eat anything when you're hungry," replied the bird. "Even vetch can be delicious when there's nothing else."

After their quick meal they set off again, and the following morning they reached the sea. The kind bird set Pinocchio down on the beach and flew off again without even waiting to be thanked.

The beach was crowded with people staring out to sea, shouting and waving their arms about.

"What's going on?" Pinocchio asked an old lady.

"A poor man came here recently, looking for his son," she explained. "He insisted on trying to cross the sea, but he's only got a little rowing boat, and it's ever so rough today. We think he's about to go under..."

"Where is he?" asked Pinocchio.

"Over there," said the old lady, pointing to a dinghy. It was so far out to sea that it looked like a nutshell with a toy figure aboard it.

Pinocchio peered at the tiny craft, then let out a shrill cry. "It's him!" he yelled. "It's my father!"

The little boat kept disappearing from view behind the huge waves only to reappear moments later. Pinocchio, who'd scrambled onto a large rock on the water's edge, was yelling his father's name, frantically waving with his cap and his grubby old handkerchief. And it looked as if Geppetto had recognized his son, despite the distance, because he took off his own hat and waved back, signalling that he wanted to return to shore but couldn't manage against such a rough sea.

All of a sudden the boat disappeared under a gigantic wave. Everyone waited with baited breath, but this time it did not reappear.

"Poor fellow!" sighed the fishermen watching from the beach. Muttering prayers under their breath, they turned to go home.

All of a sudden they
heard a desperate wail.
Looking back, they saw a
figure dive into the sea, shouting,
"I'll save you, Father!"

Pinocchio, being made entirely of
wood, floated easily, and he swam
like a fish. The crowd watched him
battle against the waves. Every time
he seemed to have drowned, they'd
spot an arm or a leg sticking out of
the water again, further and further
from land. Eventually they lost sight
of him altogether.

"Poor lad!" sighed the fishermen.
Muttering more prayers under their
breath, they turned to go home.

CHaPTER 24

Sustained by the hope that he might save his father's life, Pinocchio swam all night long. And what a night it was! The rain and hail came down in sheets. Thunder boomed. Lightning lit up the sea like daylight.

At dawn, Pinocchio spotted an island close by. He strained every muscle to reach it but was constantly thwarted by the waves, which crashed down on him relentlessly and tossed him around like a twig or a piece of straw. In the end, by a stroke of luck, the mightiest wave of all lifted him up and threw him onto one of the island's beaches.

Pinocchio hit the sand with such force that all his ribs and joints creaked, but he didn't mind.

Another close shave, he thought. I've been lucky again.

Gradually the sky cleared. The sun came out in all its glory. The sea became as flat as a millpond. Pinocchio took off his clothes and spread them out to dry. Then he turned to the sea, hoping that somewhere in that vast expanse he might spot a man in a tiny boat. But, try as he might, he could see nothing but sky, water and the occasional sail of a large ship, so far away that it looked like a fly crawling along the horizon.

I wish I knew the name of this place, he thought to himself, and whether the locals are good people and not in the habit of hanging boys from the branches of large trees. But there's nobody here to ask.

The idea of being all on his own on that large, uninhabited island made him feel so lonely that he'd have burst into tears if he hadn't suddenly seen, not far from the shore, a large fish swimming with its head sticking out of the water.

Pinocchio wasn't sure quite how to address a fish, so he just called out loudly, "Excuse me, Mr Fish, could you spare me a minute of your time?"

"I'd be delighted," replied the fish, who was actually a dolphin and the pleasantest creature you could hope to meet in all the ocean.

"Could you tell me if there are any towns or villages on this island, where a person could eat and not get eaten?" Pinocchio asked.

"There most certainly are," replied the dolphin. "In fact, there's a town just near by."

"How do I get there?"

"Just follow that path to your left. You can't go wrong."

"And would you be so kind," Pinocchio went on, "as to help me with something else? Since you spend a great deal of your time in the sea, I was wondering if you'd come across a little boat with my father in it?"

"Who is your father?" asked the dolphin.

"He is the best father in the whole world," replied Pinocchio. "And I am the worst son."

"Any small craft is bound to have sunk in last night's storm."

"But what about my father?"

"By now I should think he's been swallowed up by the merciless shark that's been terrorizing our waters over the last few days."

"Is it a very large merciless shark?" Pinocchio asked. A shiver ran down his spine.

"Large?" the dolphin answered. "Let's just say it's larger than a five-storey block of flats and its mouth is so wide and deep, you could drive a steam train through it."

"Help!" squealed Pinocchio. He pulled on his clothes as fast as he could, thanked the dolphin for his help and set off down the path to the village at a pace that didn't say much for his bravery. The slightest noise made him jump and look over his shoulder, where he expected to see a merciless shark as big as a five-storey building, with a steam engine hanging out of its mouth.

After half an hour he came to a place called Busy Bee village, where the streets were buzzing with activity.

Everybody seemed to be hard at work. You couldn't have found a single idler in this village, no matter how hard you looked.

Oh dear, the lazy puppet thought. This is definitely not my kind of place. I wasn't born to work.

By this time he was beginning to feel very hungry indeed – he hadn't eaten a thing in twenty-four hours, not even a plate of vetch.

Pinocchio was ashamed to beg because his father had always told him that the only people who had the right to ask for charity were the aged and the infirm. If the young and fit went hungry because they wouldn't work, Geppetto used to say, so much the worse for them.

Just then a tired, sweaty man tramped by, pulling two cartloads of coal all by himself. Pinocchio went up to him.

"Excuse me, sir, but I'm ever so hungry," he mumbled, his eyes lowered in shame. "Could you spare me a penny to buy some food?"

"I'll do more than that," the coalman replied. "I'll pay you fourpence if you help me pull these carts home."

"Not likely!" Pinocchio exclaimed, offended. "I've never pulled a cart in my life. I'm not a donkey."

"Good for you," replied the coalman. "In that case, may I suggest you dine on a couple of slices of your pride – and watch you don't give yourself indigestion."

A few minutes later a builder came by, carrying a bucket of cement on his shoulder.

"Could you spare a penny for a poor boy who's feeling faint with hunger?" Pinocchio asked.

"Of course," replied the builder. "Come and help me carry this cement, and instead of one coin I'll give you five."

"But cement is heavy," Pinocchio pointed out. "I'll get tired."

"If you don't want to get tired," the builder replied, "you can carry on feeling faint instead, and I hope you enjoy it."

Over the next half an hour another twenty people passed by, and Pinocchio asked them all for money, only to hear them say, "Aren't you ashamed? Go and find some work. Earn your own money."

Finally a woman came by, carrying two water jugs. Pinocchio was dying of thirst.

"Madam," he asked, "could I possibly drink a little of your water?"

"Go ahead, my child," the woman replied kindly, putting the jugs down on the pavement.

Once Pinocchio had drunk like a fish, he wiped his mouth, muttering, "Well, that's slaked my thirst. I just wish I could satisfy my hunger too."

"If you help me carry one of these jugs home, I'll give you some bread," said the good woman.

Pinocchio eyed the water jug suspiciously, and said nothing.

"And a plate of cauliflower with vinegar dressing," added the lady.

Pinocchio still eyed the jug, but didn't commit himself.

"And after the cauliflower you can have some sugared almonds."

The promise of this last delicacy decided him. "All right, then," he said. "I'll carry it home for you."

The jug was too heavy for Pinocchio to carry in his arms, so he had to balance it on his head. When they reached the woman's house, she sat Pinocchio down at a small table, already laid for one, and presented him with the bread, the cauliflower and the sugared almonds.

Pinocchio did not eat so much as guzzle. His stomach felt like a town centre that had been left deserted for five months. When his hunger pangs had abated slightly, he looked up to thank his benefactress. But as he gazed into her face, all he could utter was a gasp of amazement. He froze with his fork mid-air, his eyes wide open and his mouth still full of bread and cauliflower.

"Why are you looking at me like that?" the kind lady laughed.

"It's just that ..." Pinocchio stammered, "you look like ... you remind me of ... the voice ... the eyes ... the blue hair... Oh, my darling, darling fairy! Please say it's you... Don't make me cry again! If you knew how much I've cried, how much I've suffered..." And with that, Pinocchio fell sobbing to his knees and flung his arms around the legs of the mysterious woman.

Chapter 25

At first the woman insisted that she was not the blue-haired fairy. Then – when she realized Pinocchio really had seen through her disguise – she admitted the truth.

"You little rascal!" she laughed. "How did you guess it was me?"

"My heart told me," Pinocchio answered.

"Last time you saw me I was a little girl," she reminded him. "Now I'm a woman. I'm old enough to be your mother."

"I know," said Pinocchio, "and I'm pleased. Now I can call you Mummy. I've always longed to have a mother like everyone else," he added, "but how did you manage to grow up so fast?"

"That's a secret."

"Tell me, I beg of you! I want to grow up too. Look at me: I'm still not much bigger than a splinter."

"You cannot grow up," the fairy replied.

"Why not?"

"Because puppets never do. Puppets are born puppets, live as puppets, and die as puppets."

"I'm sick of being a puppet!" Pinocchio cried, beating himself on the head in frustration. "It's high time I became a normal person."

"And so you will, if you can earn it..." the fairy promised.

"Will I?" cried Pinocchio. "Really? How?"

"It's easy: learn to behave."

"Don't I already behave?"

"Great heavens, no!" the fairy exclaimed. "Well-behaved boys do as they're told..."

"...and I never do," admitted Pinocchio.

"Well-behaved boys study. Well-behaved boys work..."

"...while I do as little as I can," said Pinocchio.

"Well-behaved boys always tell the truth..."

"...while I tell fibs."

"Well-behaved boys do their best at school..."

"...while school gives me a stomach-ache – but I'll change."

"Is that a promise?" asked the fairy.

"It is. I want to be good. I want my father to be proud of me. Poor Father," Pinocchio sighed. "I wonder where he is now!"

"I don't know," replied the fairy.

"Will I ever see him again?" Pinocchio asked.

"I believe that you will," replied the fairy. "In fact, I'm certain."

Pinocchio seized the fairy's hands and covered them in such an avalanche of kisses that he seemed to have gone quite mad. When he finally stopped, he looked up at her lovingly.

"So you never really died?"

"It doesn't look like it, does it?"

"If you only knew how I felt when I saw the words 'Here lies...'"

"I do know," the fairy said, "and that's why I've forgiven you. Your pain was so real that I knew you were good at heart. When children have a good heart, even if they're a bit naughty and spoilt there's still hope that they'll mend. That's why I came all this way to find you. I will be your mother," she went on.

"Hooray!" yelled Pinocchio, jumping up and down.

"You will behave, and you will do as I say."

"Of course!" Pinocchio agreed eagerly.

"You'll start school tomorrow."

Pinocchio's new zeal began to wane.

"Then you'll find a trade that interests you..."

Pinocchio stared at the floor and muttered something under his breath.

"What was that?" the fairy asked sharply.

"I was just saying," the puppet reluctantly replied, "that it seems a bit late to start school now."

"It is never too late to learn."

"But I don't want to work..."

"And why is that, pray?"

"Because," Pinocchio mumbled, "it's too much of an effort."

"Child," said the fairy, "with that attitude you'll end up in one of two places: prison or hospital. Everybody, rich or poor, has the duty to do something. Sloth is a terrible disease, which has to be dealt with in childhood. In adults it's incurable."

Pinocchio was impressed. He stopped staring at his toes and looked up at the good fairy.

"I'll work," he said. "I'll study. I'll do everything you tell me. I'm tired of being a puppet. I want to be a real boy, no matter what it takes. You promised I could, didn't you?"

"I promised," agreed the fairy. "But now it's up to you."

chapter 26

The very next day Pinocchio started at the local school.

You can imagine the children's reaction when they saw a wooden puppet walk into their classroom. They hooted with laughter. They teased him mercilessly: they pulled off his hat; they yanked at his jacket; they tried to draw a moustache under his nose. Somebody even tried to tie strings to his hands and feet, to make him dance.

For a while Pinocchio ignored them, but eventually he lost patience.

"Listen," he said sternly, addressing the worst offenders. "I didn't come here to be your clown. I respect other people, and I want to be respected too."

"Listen to him! He talks like a book!" the rascals yelled, laughing their heads off. One of the cheekiest reached out to grab the end of Pinocchio's nose, but

he wasn't quick enough. Before he knew it, the puppet had stretched out from under his desk and kicked him on the shin.

"Ouch!" the boy yelled, rubbing his bruise. "His feet are hard!"

"So are his elbows!" squealed another lad, who'd just paid for his taunting with a dig in the stomach.

Needless to say, these two acts of violence won Pinocchio the admiration and friendship of every boy in the school. They all made a tremendous fuss of him and liked him immensely.

The teacher was pleased with his new pupil, because he was intelligent, attentive and studious – always the first to arrive and the last to leave. His only weakness was that he hung around with too wide a group of friends, quite a few of whom were well-known for their lack of enthusiasm for learning.

The teacher would warn him about this every day. So would the good fairy. "Sooner or later," she would say, "your schoolmates' idleness will rub off on you. You could end up in real trouble."

"Don't you worry about me," Pinocchio would reply, shrugging and tapping his forehead in a gesture that meant: "I've got plenty up here."

One fine day, while Pinocchio was on his way to school, he ran into a large gang of his friends. They crowded round him, yelling, "Have you heard the news?"

"What news?" Pinocchio asked.

"They've sighted a shark as big as a mountain off a beach not far away from here."

"Have they?" said Pinocchio. "I wonder if it's the same one that was around when my poor father drowned."

1 + 1 = 2

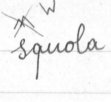

"We're off to see it," they said. "Are you coming?"

"No. I'm going to school."

"Oh, come on," they told him. "School can wait till tomorrow. One or two lessons aren't going to make any difference."

"But what about the teacher?"

"Let him grumble. That's what he's paid for."

"And my mother?"

"Mothers don't know anything," replied the rascals.

"I do have a reason for wanting to see this shark," Pinocchio said, "but I'll go after school."

"You great idiot!" laughed one of the gang. "Do you think a fish that big is going to hang about waiting for you? When he's bored of this bit of sea, he'll be off, and that'll be the last we see of him."

"How long does it take to get there?" the puppet asked.

"An hour," they replied, "there and back."

"All right then," Pinocchio agreed. "The last one to the beach is a donkey!" he whooped, and the whole gang began to career across the fields, with their schoolbooks under their arms.

Pinocchio stayed in the lead the whole way. He ran like the wind. From time to time, he looked over his shoulder and laughed at his friends, trailing far behind. He thought they looked funny, covered in dust, puffing along with their tongues hanging out. The poor boy sped on, with no idea of the new terrors and disasters that lay ahead.

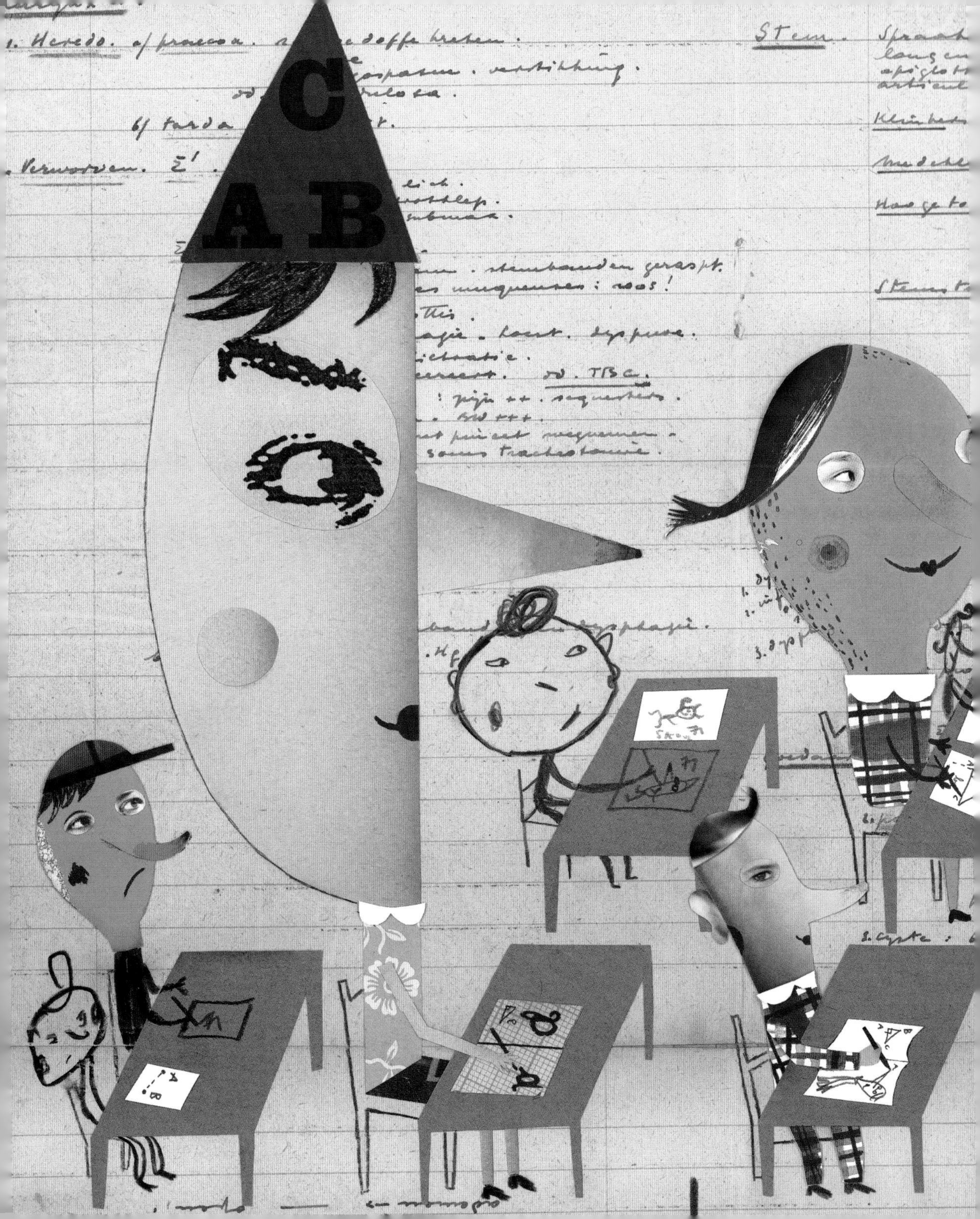
C
A B

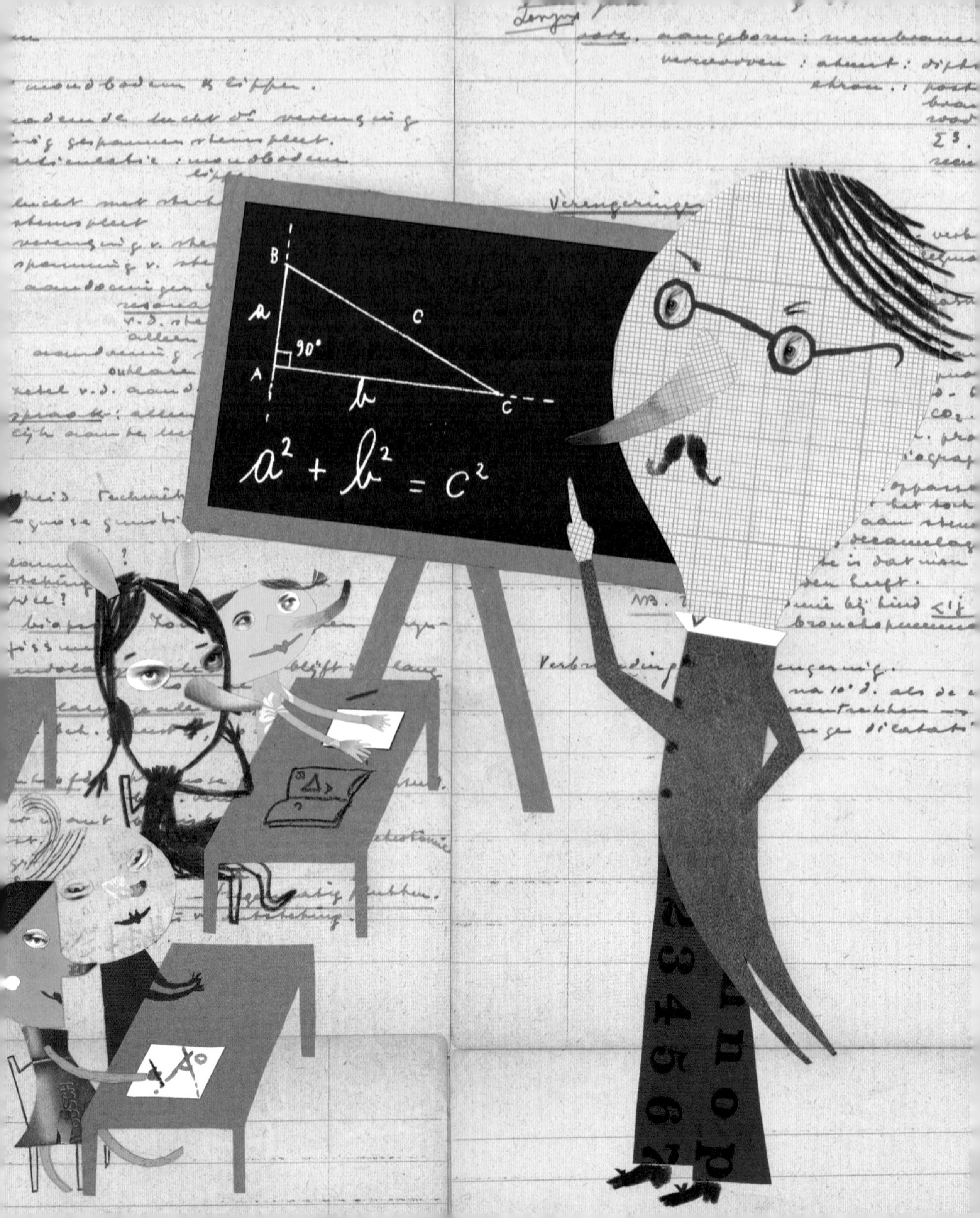

B
a
c
90°
A
b
C
a² + b² = c²

CHAPTER 27

The moment he got to the beach, Pinocchio looked out to sea. There was no sign of the shark. The water was as flat as a giant mirror.

"Where is it?" he asked his companions.

"It must have nipped round the corner for some breakfast," one of them tittered.

"Maybe it's tucked up in bed having a nap," laughed another.

Pinocchio suddenly realized that the whole shark story was a practical joke. It didn't go down well.

"Very clever," he growled. "And what is the point of all this?"

"To make you miss school!" they chorused. "Aren't you ashamed?" they said. "You're such a swot – you're never late; you do all your homework..."

"What's it to you if I work hard?"

"You show us up."

"What do you mean?"

"People like you make people like us look bad. And we don't want to look bad – we've got our pride too, you know."

"So what do you want me to do?"

"Be like us. Hate school and lessons and teachers – the Three Great Enemies."

"And what if I won't? What if I like studying?"

"Then we'll send you to Coventry. And we'll make you pay for it."

"If you weren't so pathetic," Pinocchio said with a shake of the head, "you'd make me laugh."

"Hey! Bighead!" the largest of the boys shouted, right in the puppet's face. "What makes you so full of yourself? We're not afraid of you. Remember you're on your own. There are seven of us."

"Like the seven deadly sins," Pinocchio replied.

"Did you hear that?" yelled the boy. "He called us deadly sins!"

"You'd better say you're sorry," they said, "or we'll make you..."

"Ha, ha, ha!" sang Pinocchio, mocking them.

"You'll be sorry, Pinocchio."

"Ha, ha, ha!"

"We'll give you a good thrashing."

"Ha, ha, ha!"

"You'll go home with a bloody nose."

"Ha, ha, ha!"

"I'll give you 'Ha, ha, ha!'" yelled the boldest of the urchins. "Take that!" And he punched Pinocchio on the side of the head.

The puppet, as you might expect, retaliated with a punch of his own, and in an instant the fight turned into a free-for-all.

Although he was only one against seven, Pinocchio defended himself valiantly. He used his hard wooden feet to such good effect that his enemies stayed at a respectful distance, and whenever he made contact with a shin or an ankle, he always left a bruise as a souvenir.

The gang, frustrated at not being able to confront the puppet at close quarters, opted for aerial bombardment. They untied their bundles of schoolbooks and began to pelt Pinocchio with grammars and

dictionaries, maths books and Histories of the Nation. But the puppet had very quick reactions: he always managed to duck, and the books sailed harmlessly over his head. They splashed into the sea, where the fish mistook them for food and gathered round in great numbers to sample a title-page or a dust cover, but after the first nibble they spat the paper out with expressions that said, "Most inferior. We're used to better than this."

As the battle raged more and more fiercely, a large crab came out of the water and slowly worked his way up the beach.

"Stop it this minute, you wicked children!" he shouted, in a voice that sounded like a trombone with a head cold. "This sort of thing always ends in tears."

The poor animal might as well have been talking to the wind. Only Pinocchio turned to scowl at him.

"Stop moaning, you old bore," he said rudely. "You'd do better to go to bed with a hot drink and cure that cold of yours."

At this point Pinocchio's enemies, who had run out of ammunition, noticed the puppet's own bundle of books and pounced on it in a flash. Among Pinocchio's schoolbooks was a large hardback volume called *The Principles of Arithmetic*. Its title gives a fair indication of its weight. This was the book that one of these ruffians chose to fling at Pinocchio's head as hard as he could. But instead of hitting the puppet, *Principles* connected with the temple of one of the gang, who immediately turned white as a sheet. He stammered, "Help me, Mummy, I'm dying..." and collapsed onto the sand.

At the sight of that small prone body, the terrified schoolboys scattered. The only person left standing on the beach was Pinocchio. Although he too was weak with fear, he ran to wet his handkerchief in the sea and began to dab his schoolmate's temple, sobbing and calling the boy's name.

"Eugene, Eugene!" he cried. "Open your eyes. Why won't you answer me? It wasn't me who hurt you, honestly it wasn't... Open your eyes, Eugene... If you don't open your eyes, I'll die too. Oh God, how can I ever go back home now? How can I face my mother? What will become of me? Oh, how I wish I'd gone to school! Why did I go with that lot? The teacher kept telling me to stay away from them, and so did my mother, but I'm so pig-headed I won't listen to a word anyone says. I always do exactly as I please, then I end up regretting it. That's why my whole life has been nothing but trouble. Oh God, what will become of me?"

Pinocchio carried on wailing and beating his brow, in between making desperate attempts to wake Eugene. Then he heard the dull thud of approaching footsteps. He turned round and saw two policemen.

"What are you doing down there on the ground?" they asked Pinocchio.

"I'm helping my friend."

"Isn't he well?"

"No."

"He certainly isn't!" exclaimed the policemen who had bent over to examine Eugene. "This boy has been struck on the temple. Who did it?"

"It wasn't me," breathed the puppet, hardly able to speak.

"If it wasn't you, who was it?"

"It wasn't me," Pinocchio repeated.

"What was he hit with?"

"This," said Pinocchio, showing *Principles of Arithmetic* to the policemen.

"And who does this book belong to?"

"Me."

"Right, that's all we need. Stand up and come with us."

"But..."

"Come with us."

"But I'm innocent!"

"Come with us."

Before leaving, the policemen hailed some passing fishermen and told them to take the wounded boy home and care for him.

"We'll be back to see him tomorrow," the policemen said. Then they turned to Pinocchio, putting him between the two of them.

"Quick march, or you'll be sorry."

Pinocchio didn't dare argue. Flanked by the two officers, he walked down the path that led to the village. He was so shocked that he barely knew what was happening. The whole thing felt like some terrible nightmare. His eyes

were seeing double. His legs were shaking. His mouth was so dry he couldn't speak. And yet, even in this confused, numb state, he was aware of a sharp pain piercing his heart: he was going to have to walk right past the kind fairy's house, escorted by two policemen. He would rather be dead.

They were about to go into the village, when a gust of wind blew Pinocchio's hat off his head. It landed a few yards away.

"Can I go and get it?" Pinocchio asked the policemen.

"All right, but be quick about it," they replied.

The puppet walked over to the hat. He picked it up, but, instead of putting it back on his head, he clenched it between his teeth and shot off towards the beach like a bullet from a gun. The policemen, realizing he was going to be very hard to catch, unleashed a large mastiff – a champion sprinter. Pinocchio ran fast, but the mastiff ran faster. The villagers all came to their windows or crowded onto the road to watch the gripping race. But they never did find out who won, because Pinocchio and his pursuer kicked up such a cloud of dust that within minutes nobody could see a thing.

chapter 28

In the course of that desperate pursuit, there was one terrible moment when Pinocchio thought all was lost. Alidoro (for that was the mastiff's name) had almost caught up with him. Pinocchio could hear the fearsome brute panting right behind him. He could feel his hot breath on the back of his neck.

Luckily they were almost at the beach. As soon as Pinocchio got close to the sea, he performed a leap worthy of any frog and landed in the water. Alidoro couldn't swim, and the last thing he wanted to do was follow Pinocchio in, but he'd built up so much speed that he couldn't stop himself crashing into the waves. The poor dog floundered about, trying to keep afloat, but the more he struggled, the more he sank.

When his head surfaced for a moment, his eyes were rolling in terror.

"I'm drowning!" he barked. "I'm drowning!"

"Good!" Pinocchio retorted from a safe distance.

"Help me, Pinocchio! Don't let me die!" the dog begged.

The puppet, who was kind at heart, couldn't help feeling sorry for his pursuer.

"If I save you," he called, "do you promise to stop chasing me?"

"I promise!" the dog howled, "I promise! But hurry! Another minute and I'll be dead..."

Pinocchio hesitated. Then he remembered his father telling him that good deeds are always rewarded, so he swam over to Alidoro, grabbed him by the tail and dragged him to the safety of the beach.

The poor creature was too weak to stand. He'd swallowed so much sea water that he'd swollen up like a beach-ball. Pinocchio, however, thought it best not to take anything for granted, so he dived back into the water. As he swam off, he shouted to his new friend, "Goodbye, Alidoro. Have a good trip back. My regards to your family."

"Goodbye, Pinocchio," replied the dog. "Thank you for saving my life. One good turn deserves another. If I ever get the chance, I'll do something for you."

Pinocchio carried on swimming, keeping close to the shore, until he felt he'd reached a safe place. Looking towards land, he saw a kind of cave in some rocks. A long trail of smoke curled from its mouth.

"There's no smoke without fire," he said to himself. "Good. I'll go in there, get dry and warm, and then ... and then we'll see."

His mind made up, he swam towards the cliffs. Just as he was about to climb out of the water, he felt something rise up beneath him, lifting him into the air. He tried to get away, but it was too late. He was amazed to find himself inside a large net, surrounded by a squirming mass of fish of all shapes and sizes, flipping about like so many lost souls.

At the same time he saw a fisherman come out of the cave. He was so very, very ugly that he looked like a sea-monster. Where most fishermen have hair, he had a thick clump of grass. His skin was green. His eyes were green. His beard – which was green – was so long that it reached down to his toes. He looked a bit like a large lizard standing on its hind legs.

The fisherman hauled the net out of the water.

"Fish for dinner again!" he exclaimed to himself, with obvious delight.

Hearing these words, Pinocchio cheered up a little. At least I'm not a fish, he thought.

The big green man carried the net into the cave. Inside it was dark and smoky. In the centre bubbled a large pan of cooking oil, which stank so badly that it took Pinocchio's breath away.

"Now to sort the catch," said the fisherman. He delved into the net with a hand so large that it looked like a spade, and pulled out a handful of fish.

"Now that's what I call mullet," he said, sniffing them carefully before slinging them into a large empty hollow in the rock. He repeated this procedure several times.

"Now that's what I call hake," he said greedily.

"Now that's what I call a halibut."

"Now that's what I call a sole."

"Now that's what I call a skate."

"Now that's what I call anchovies."

The hake, the halibut, the sole, the skate and the anchovies all joined the mullet in the stone sink. Pinocchio was at the very bottom of the net.

"Now that's..." began the fisherman, as he pulled him out. His green eyes opened wide in wonder.

"What on earth do I call this?" he cried, sounding almost scared. "I've never seen a fish like this before."

He examined the puppet closely, turning him over and over.

"I know," he decided finally. "It must be some kind of a crab."

Pinocchio didn't appreciate being mistaken for a crustacean.

"Who are you calling a crab?" he piped up, resentfully. "I'll have you know that I'm a puppet, and this is no way to treat me."

"A puppet?" the fisherman said. "I don't mind admitting I've never come across a puppet fish before. All the better. I love new flavours."

"New flavours!" cried Pinocchio. "How many times do I have to tell you I'm not a fish? Can't you hear me talk and reason, like you do?"

"True," agreed the fisherman, "and since you're a fish that's able to speak and reason, I'm going to treat you with due respect."

"In what way?" asked Pinocchio, warily.

"As a token of my unique admiration and friendship for you, I'll let you choose how to be eaten. Would you like to be pan-fried, or stewed in tomato sauce?"

"I'd rather you set me free and let me go home."

"You're joking! Do you think I'd miss the chance to taste such an unusual fish? It's not every day we catch puppet fish round here, you know. Very well, if you won't decide, I'll do it for you: I'll fry you, with all the others. You'll enjoy it – it's always nice to have company."

The unfortunate puppet burst into tears. "If only I'd gone to school!" he wailed. "But no, I listened to my friends, and now look where it's got me!"

Pinocchio was squirming about like an eel, making valiant efforts to slip out of the fisherman's grip. The green man picked up a strong reed, tied him up by the hands and feet, like a sausage, and threw him into the stone sink with the others. Then he fetched a large wooden bowl full of flour. He dipped the fish in it, one by one, before throwing them into the frying-pan.

The first to sizzle in the hot oil were the mullet, followed by the hake, then the halibut, the sole, the skate and the anchovies. Then, finally, it was Pinocchio's turn. With death (and what a death!) staring him in the face, the puppet started to shake so violently that he could no longer speak. He tried to plead with his eyes, but the green fisherman paid no attention. He rolled Pinocchio in the flour five or six times, until he looked like a plaster cast of a puppet. Then he gripped him firmly by the head. And then...

CHAPTER 29

Just as the fisherman was about to throw Pinocchio into the frying-pan, a large dog bounded into the cave, attracted by the smell of frying.

"Go away!" the green man yelled at him, still holding the floury puppet by his head.

But the dog was very hungry indeed. He whined and wagged his tail, as if to say, "Just one mouthful of fish and I'll leave you in peace."

"I said go away!" the green man repeated, aiming a kick at the animal.

Now, this dog was not the type to let himself be ordered about, especially when he was famished. He turned on the fisherman and growled, baring a terrifying set of fangs.

Just then a little voice rang out in the cave: "Save me, Alidoro! He's about to pan-fry me!"

The dog immediately recognized Pinocchio's voice, and realized in amazement that it was coming from the floury bundle in the fisherman's hand. He leapt up, seized Pinocchio gently in his teeth and then ran out of the cave and away.

The fisherman had been looking forward to his rare fish and was furious at having it snatched away. He tried to give chase, but after only a few steps was overcome by a fit of coughing and forced to turn back.

Alidoro reached the path that led to the village. He stopped and put his friend Pinocchio carefully on the ground.

"Alidoro! I'll never be able to thank you enough," said the puppet.

"You're welcome," replied the dog. "You saved my life, and I returned the favour. What are we in this world for, if not to help one another?"

"But what on earth brought you to that cave?" Pinocchio asked.

"I was lying half dead on the sand," Alidoro explained, "when the sea breeze wafted over the smell of frying. It made me hungry, so I followed it. If I'd got there a minute later..."

"Don't even talk about it!" cried Pinocchio, shuddering. "If you'd got there a minute later, I wouldn't be standing here talking to you: I'd have been fried, eaten and digested. It gives me the shivers just to think about it."

Laughing, Alidoro extended his right paw to the puppet. Pinocchio shook it warmly, as a bond of friendship.

Then they parted company: the dog set off home, while Pinocchio waited till he was alone, then walked over to a nearby hut, where an old man was sitting at his front door enjoying the sunshine.

"Excuse me, sir," said Pinocchio. "Have you by any chance heard anything about a boy called Eugene getting hit on the head?"

"Yes. Some fishermen brought him to this hut, and now—"

"He's dead," Pinocchio interrupted miserably.

"Not at all. He's alive and well. In fact, he's already gone home."

"Thank goodness!" Pinocchio cried, jumping for joy. "So he wasn't badly hurt?"

"He wasn't, but he could have been. He could even have died; he had a heavy book thrown at him, you know."

"Who by?"

"A schoolmate of his: a boy called Pinocchio."

"Who's he?" asked Pinocchio innocently.

"They say he's a thug and a layabout, without a streak of good in him."

"That's not true!" Pinocchio exclaimed.

"Do you know him?" the old man asked curiously.

"Just by sight," Pinocchio replied hurriedly.

"What do you make of him, then?"

"He's always struck me as an excellent sort: well-behaved, diligent, considerate, kind to his family..."

As Pinocchio was blithely assembling this list of lies, he happened to touch his nose. To his horror, he realized that it had grown by at least a couple of centimetres.

"Please, sir, ignore what I've just said!" he cried. "I know Pinocchio very well and can confirm that he is disobedient and lazy – an incorrigible scoundrel who bunks off school to make trouble with his friends."

As soon as he'd uttered these words, his nose shrank back to its normal size.

"And by the way," the old man suddenly asked, "why are you all covered in white?"

"I accidentally brushed against some wet paint," the puppet answered, ashamed to admit that he'd been rolled in flour like a fish and almost pan-fried.

"And where have your clothes gone?"

"Some thieves stole them... You couldn't possibly give me something to wear – just to get home in?"

"I don't have anything, my child, just a small sack which I use to keep lupin seeds in. You can have that if you want: it's over there."

Pinocchio didn't need to be asked twice. He took the empty lupin sack, cut a hole in the top and two small holes in the sides, and slipped it on like a shirt. In this scant clothing he set off for the village. But the closer he got, the more he dragged his feet, until he was almost walking backwards. He wasn't feeling very good at all about going home.

"How can I face my beloved fairy?" he asked himself out loud. "What's she going to say? Can she forgive me a second time? I'm afraid she won't be able to ... I'm sure she won't! And quite right, too – I'm an incorrigible scoundrel. I keep promising to mend my ways, and I never do."

By the time he reached the village, night had fallen. Since it was raining cats and dogs, Pinocchio went straight to the fairy's house, determined to knock on her door no matter what.

But when he got there, his courage failed him. He retreated twenty paces or so. Then he approached the door a second time, but again he lost his nerve. A third attempt had the same result. Finally, the fourth time, he took the iron knocker in his trembling hand and knocked gingerly.

He waited and waited. After half an hour, a window opened on the top floor (it was a four-storey house) and a large snail with a lantern on her head peered out.

"Who's calling, at this time of night?" she asked.

"Is the fairy at home?" the puppet asked.

"The fairy is asleep and doesn't want to be disturbed. Who is it?"

"It's me!"

"Me who?"

"Pinocchio."

"Pinocchio who?"

"The puppet who lives with the fairy."

"Oh, I see," said the snail. "Just a moment – I'll come down and open the door."

"Hurry, do!" Pinocchio pleaded. "It's freezing out here."

"I'm a snail, child," replied the creature. "Snails never hurry."

An hour went by, then two, but the door stayed shut. Pinocchio – soaked to the skin and shivering with cold and fear – plucked up his courage and knocked again, a little more loudly.

A third-floor window opened and the snail appeared.

"I've been waiting for two hours!" Pinocchio called up to her.

"I'm a snail, child," the gentle soul replied. "Snails never hurry."

The window closed again.

Soon after this, the village clock struck midnight, then one, then two o'clock, but the door stayed as firmly bolted as ever. At last Pinocchio lost all patience. In a fit of temper he seized the knocker, meaning to make such a racket that the whole building would be roused. But the knocker, which was made of iron, suddenly turned into a live eel, slipped through his fingers and disappeared into the stream of rainwater running down the middle of the street.

"So that's it, is it?" yelled Pinocchio, blind with fury. "Well, if the knocker's gone, I can still use my feet!"

He stepped back and aimed a tremendous kick at the front door. It was such a powerful blow that his foot sank into the wood and, try as he might, he couldn't pull it out again. It was stuck as fast as a nail.

Poor Pinocchio! He was forced to spend a very uncomfortable night with one foot off the ground.

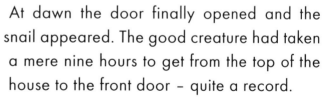

At dawn the door finally opened and the snail appeared. The good creature had taken a mere nine hours to get from the top of the house to the front door – quite a record.

"What are you doing with your foot in the door?" she asked, laughing.

"I had an accident," Pinocchio replied. "See if you can set me free, dearest snail."

"It's going to take carpentry to get you out of there, child. Snails don't do carpentry."

"Could you ask the fairy?"

"The fairy is sleeping and doesn't want to be disturbed."

"But what do you expect me to do, stuck here all day long?"

"You could count ants..."

"Could you at least bring me something to eat? I'm starving."

"Right away!" said the snail.

Three and a half hours later she returned with a silver tray balanced on her head. On the tray was a loaf of bread, a whole roast chicken and four ripe apricots.

"Breakfast, with the compliments of the fairy," she said.

At the sight of so much delicious food, the puppet cheered up considerably. But imagine his disappointment when he tried to eat and discovered that the bread was made out of plaster, the chicken of cardboard and the four apricots of alabaster!

Pinocchio felt like crying and giving up in desperation. He felt like throwing the tray and its contents on the floor. What he actually did, either through sorrow or hunger, was fall to the ground in a faint.

When he came to, he was lying on a sofa, with the fairy at his side.

"I'll forgive you once more," she said, "but you'd better not get up to your old tricks!"

Pinocchio swore to behave and to do his schoolwork.

He kept his word for the whole of the rest of the year. When the end-of-year exams came round, he got the best mark in the school. In fact, he had been such a model child in every way that the fairy called him to her and said, "Tomorrow your wish will come true. Tomorrow you will stop being a wooden puppet and turn into a real boy." Pinocchio went wild with joy at this long-awaited news.

The fairy had arranged a party the following day, to celebrate the great event. All Pinocchio's friends and schoolmates were to be invited. The fairy's cook had

already prepared two hundred cups of cocoa and four hundred sandwiches, buttered inside and out. It promised to be a wonderful event, but...

In the life of a puppet there is always a "but", and it ends up ruining everything.

chapter 30

Pinocchio asked the fairy if he could go round to his friends' houses to invite them in person.

"Of course," said the fairy, "but come home before it gets dark."

"I'll be back within the hour," the puppet replied.

"Be sure you are, Pinocchio. Children are always making promises, but as often as not they don't keep them."

"But I'm not like other children – I always keep my word."

"We'll see," said the fairy. "Of course, if you did disobey, you'd soon be sorry."

"Why?"

"Because boys who don't listen to their elders always end up in trouble."

"I've noticed that!" Pinocchio laughed. "But I'm not making that mistake again!"

"We'll see," said the fairy.

Pinocchio didn't insist on this point. He kissed the good fairy, who was like a mother to him, then skipped out of the house. In less than an hour he'd visited all his friends. Some accepted his invitation with pleasure. Others had to be convinced, but when they found out that the sandwiches were to be buttered both inside and out, they said, "Oh all right then, just to please you."

Now, you should know that Pinocchio had a best friend at school. He was called Romeo, but was always known as "Lampwick" because he was as skinny as the new wick in an oil-lamp. Lampwick was the naughtiest, laziest boy in the whole school, but Pinocchio was very fond of him. In fact, he'd gone to Lampwick's house first, but his friend wasn't in. He went back a little later, but still no Lampwick. He even tried a third time, with the same result.

Where could he be? Pinocchio searched everywhere. Eventually he found his friend hiding in a farmhouse porch.

"What are you doing here?" Pinocchio asked.

"I'm waiting for midnight, then I'm off..."

"Where are you going?"

"A long, long way away."

"I've just been to your place three times, looking for you."

"Why, what did you want?"

"Haven't you heard my wonderful news?"

"No, what is it?"

"Tomorrow I won't be a puppet any more. I'll be a real boy, like the rest of you."

"Glad to hear it."

"So you're invited to a party at my house tomorrow."

"I told you: I'm leaving tonight."

"At what time?"

"Midnight, you chump!"

"Where are you going?"

"I'm emigrating to the most wonderful country in the world. A fantastic place!"

"What's it called?"

"Toyland. Why don't you come too?"

"I'm not going anywhere."

"You're making a mistake, Pinocchio. You'll regret it, believe me. It's the perfect place for children. There are no schools, and no teachers, and no books. It's a kind of paradise where nobody has to study at all. There's no school on Thursdays, and every week in Toyland is made up of six Thursdays and one Sunday. The holidays begin on the first of January and end on the last day of December – just imagine! It's my kind of country. All civilized nations should work like that."

"But what do children do all day long in Toyland?"

"They just play and have fun until they drop. Then they go to bed, and the next morning they start all over again. How does that sound?"

"Hmm..." was all Pinocchio said, but he shook his head in a way that meant, "It sounds pretty good."

"So do you want to come with me?" asked Lampwick. "Make your mind up."

"No, no, definitely not," Pinocchio answered. "I promised the fairy I'd be good, and I want to keep my word. In fact, I'd better be going – it's almost dark. Goodbye, Lampwick. Have a good journey."

"Where are you going in such a hurry?"

"Home. My fairy wants me to be back before dark."

"Stay another couple of minutes."

"I'll be late."

"Just two minutes!"

"But what if the fairy scolds me?"

"Let her. She'll stop when she's finished," said his naughty friend.

"How are you travelling? Alone?" asked the puppet.

"Alone?" scoffed Lampwick. "There will be more than a hundred of us!"

"Are you on foot?"

"No, there's a carriage coming to pick us up at midnight."

"I wish it was midnight now."

"Why?"

"Because I'd like to watch you all set off."

"Stay a bit longer and you will."

"No, I've got to get home."

"Wait two more minutes."

"I've waited too long already. The fairy will be worried."

"Poor fairy! What's she worried about – that you'll get eaten by bats?"

"Tell me," Pinocchio asked suddenly. "Are you absolutely sure there are no schools in that country?"

"Not a single one."

"And that no one ever has to study?"

"Never, ever, ever."

"What an amazing place!" Pinocchio sighed dreamily. "What a place! I can just imagine it."

"Why don't you come?"

"It's no use trying to tempt me. I promised the fairy I'd be sensible, and I don't want to break my promise."

"Well, goodbye then, Pinocchio," Lampwick said cheerily. "Give my regards to primary education ... and secondary education too, if you happen to meet it out walking!"

"Goodbye, Lampwick. I hope the journey goes well. Have a good time and think of your old friends now and then."

The puppet took a few steps, then turned round.

"Are you quite sure," he said, "about the weeks being made up of six Thursdays and a Sunday?"

"I'm certain of it."

"What a great place," Pinocchio sighed again. He pulled himself together.

"Well, goodbye for real this time," he said hurriedly. "Have a great journey."

"Goodbye."

"When did you say you were leaving?"

"In two hours' time!"

"Pity. If it was only an hour, I could almost wait."

"But what about your fairy?"

"Well, I'm already late. An hour won't make any difference."

"What if she scolds you?"

"Let her," said Pinocchio. "She'll stop when she's finished."

Night had fallen while the two boys were talking. It was pitch dark. Suddenly they saw a pinprick of light in the distance. They heard a faint rumbling, like thunder, and a blast from a trumpet, so far away that it sounded like the whine of a mosquito.

"There it is!" Lampwick shouted, leaping to his feet.

"What?" Pinocchio whispered.

"My carriage. So, are you coming, yes or no?"

"Is it really true that nobody ever has to go to school?"

"Absolutely never!" Lampwick replied.

"What a great place..."

CHAPTER 31

Finally the carriage arrived, drawing up next to the two boys without a sound because its wheels were wrapped in rags.

It was pulled by twelve pairs of donkeys, all the same size but different colours. Some were grey, some white, some speckled and still others striped with great blue and yellow stripes. But the strangest thing was this: all twelve pairs (twenty-four donkeys in all) were shod not in iron, but in white leather boots.

And what about the coachman? Imagine, if you will, a small person who is almost as broad as he is tall, soft and unctuous as a pat of butter, with a rosy face, a mouth

that is always wreathed in smiles and a thin, mellifluous voice that sounds like a cat trying to get on the right side of a fellow with a pilchard.

Children always fall in love with him the moment they see him, and jostle each other to climb into his coach and be transported to that earthly paradise known to geographers as Toyland.

The carriage was already crammed with boys between the ages of eight and twelve, piled on top of each other like sardines in a tin. They were squeezed in far too tightly and could hardly breathe, but not one of them complained. The knowledge that, in a few hours' time, they would be in a land where there were no books, no schools and no teachers made them so happy and patient that they simply didn't feel the discomfort, the pushing and shoving, the hunger, the thirst and the weariness.

As soon as the carriage had stopped, the driver turned to Lampwick and gave him a sugary smile.

"Tell me, my handsome lad," he said ingratiatingly. "Would you like to come with us to the land of wonders?"

"I most certainly would," Lampwick replied.

"But I have to warn you, my charming boy, that there's no room left inside. We're quite full, as you can see."

"Never mind!" cried Lampwick. "I'll make do with the carriage shaft." And he leapt on.

"And what about you, dear lad?" the little man asked Pinocchio. "Are you coming with us or staying here?"

"I'm staying," said Pinocchio. "I want to go home. I want to go to school and do the best I can, like all good children."

"Admirable sentiments," said the coachman dryly.

"Pinocchio," called out Lampwick. "Don't be an idiot. Come with us – we'll have a whale of a time!"

"I can't."

"Come with us. We'll have a whale of a time!" shouted several voices inside the carriage.

"Come with us. We'll have a whale of a time!" chorused hundreds of voices.

"But what will my fairy say?" asked the puppet, beginning to waver.

"Stop fretting!" they replied. "Just think, where we're going we can run wild from dawn till dusk!"

Pinocchio didn't answer, but he sighed deeply. Then he sighed again. Finally he sighed for a third time and then spoke.

"Move over," he said. "I'm coming aboard."

"There isn't any room," the driver reminded him. "But to prove how much we want you with us, I'll give you my seat..."

"But what about you?"

"I'll walk."

"No, no, I can't allow that. I'd rather ride on one of these donkeys."

Pinocchio went up to the right-hand donkey of the first pair and tried to climb onto its back, but the animal turned round and shoved him in the stomach with its nose, so hard that he went flying and landed on the ground with his legs in the air.

This mishap was greeted by howls of laughter from every child in the carriage.

The little coachman, however, did not laugh. With a look of loving patience on his face he got down from the box and, pretending to give Pinocchio's stubborn donkey a kiss, bit off half the animal's right ear.

In the meantime Pinocchio had picked himself up off the ground in a blind fury. He performed one giant leap, which landed him precisely in position on the donkey's back. It was such an impressive feat that the children stopped laughing and began to applaud uproariously, shouting, "Well done, Pinocchio! Hooray for Pinocchio!"

All of a sudden the donkey reared up and threw Pinocchio into the middle of the road, right on top of a pile of gravel.

There was more laughter from the children, but the driver was not at all amused. Instead he was overcome with such affection for the restless animal that he kissed it again, and bit off half its other ear. Then he turned to Pinocchio.

"You can get back on now," he told him. "Don't be afraid – he was feeling a bit skittish, that's all. I'm sure he'll behave himself from now on. I've had a word in his ear."

Pinocchio got back on his mount and they set off at last. As the donkeys galloped and the carriage sped along the cobbled road, the puppet thought he heard a little voice talking to him.

"Poor fool!" it said ever so faintly. "You wouldn't listen to your betters, and you'll regret it."

Pinocchio looked around nervously for the speaker, but he couldn't see anybody. The donkeys were hard at work. The children were all asleep inside the speeding carriage. Lampwick was snoring, and the coachman was singing to himself, up on the box, "The whole world sleeps at night. I never sleep at all..."

After about half a mile, Pinocchio heard the voice again.

"Listen to me, you silly idiot!" it hissed. "Children who turn their back on learning always come to a bad end. I'm living proof of it. One day you'll be crying bitter tears, like I am now. But by then it will be too late."

This time the puppet really was frightened. He dismounted and went to take his donkey by the halter. Imagine how surprised he was to see that the animal was crying, just like a human being!

"Hey, Mr Coachman," he called up to the little man. "There's something odd going on. This donkey's crying."

"Let him. He can laugh when he gets married," the little man replied.

"You haven't taught him to speak, by any chance?" Pinocchio asked.

"No, but he's learnt a few words on his own. It comes of living with performing dogs for three years."

"Poor creature!" sighed Pinocchio.

"Don't waste time over a donkey's tears," the driver said. "Get back onto him and we'll be off. The night is cold and the road is long."

Pinocchio did as he was told. The carriage began to move again, and at dawn the following morning they had arrived.

Toyland was a country unlike any other. It was populated entirely by children – the oldest fourteen, the youngest just eight. The volume of happy yelling, screaming and laughing in the streets was enough to blow your head off. Everywhere you looked there were crowds of children: some playing football, others marbles or conkers; some riding on bikes, others on wooden horses. A few were playing blindman's-buff or tag. One little group was eating candyfloss, dressed in clowns' outfits. There was play-acting going on, as well as singing, cartwheels and acrobatics. Some children rolled large wooden hoops while others wandered about pretending to be generals, with paper helmets and papier-mâché swords. Everywhere children were laughing, shouting, calling to each other, clapping, whistling and imitating a hen that's just laid an egg... So intense was the uproar that the only way not to go deaf was to put cotton wool in your ears.

Every town square had a tent with a show in it, all crowded with children from morning till night. Every house was daubed with slogans such as WE LUV TOYS, NO MORE SKOOL, DOWN WITH TEETCHERS and other such triumphs of spelling.

Pinocchio, Lampwick and the other new arrivals plunged into the crowd, and they'd soon made friends with everyone. No boys had ever been happier. First hours, then days, then weeks flew by in a flash.

From time to time Pinocchio would meet Lampwick in the throng.

"This is the life!" the puppet would say.

"Was I right, or was I right?" his friend would crow. "And to think that you very nearly didn't come. You were so keen to go home to that fairy of yours and waste your time swotting! Now you'll never have to see a book or a school again, and all thanks to me. I think you'll agree I behaved like a true friend over this."

"You did, Lampwick," said Pinocchio. "I owe my happiness to you. Do you know what our old teacher used to say? He said, 'Steer clear of that good-for-nothing Lampwick. He's a Bad Influence. He'll only lead you astray.'"

"The poor fool!" sighed Lampwick, shaking his head. "I always knew he didn't like me. But I forgive him. I'm generous by nature."

"Noble soul!" Pinocchio cried. He hugged his friend, and kissed him affectionately on the forehead.

Five months flew by, in a whirl of fun and games, without a book being opened. Then, one fine morning, Pinocchio woke to a horrible surprise – one which put his nose right out of joint, as the saying goes.

CHAPTER 32

Would you like to know what surprise greeted Pinocchio that fine morning? I'll tell you.

When he woke up, he scratched his head in a sleepy way. As he did this he noticed, to his amazement, that his ears had grown at least ten centimetres.

You, my young readers, will be aware that ever since birth Pinocchio's ears had been tiny – so tiny, in fact, as to be quite invisible to the naked eye. You should, therefore, have no difficulty imagining his shock at their overnight transformation into ears the size of canoe paddles.

Pinocchio looked around for a mirror but couldn't find one. He filled the bathroom sink with water and leant over it to examine his reflection. A horrible sight met his eyes: his face was decorated, on either side, with a magnificent pair of donkey's ears!

Pinocchio burst into tears. He began screaming and banging his head against the wall in desperation. But the more he cried, the more his ears grew. They even sprouted hairs at the top.

A pretty squirrel, who lived on the floor above, heard his piercing cries and went into his room to investigate. Seeing Pinocchio in such a state, she asked kindly, "What's wrong, my dear housemate?"

"I'm ill, pretty squirrel," replied Pinocchio. "I've been struck down by a very frightening disease... Can you take my temperature?"

"I'll try," she replied.

The squirrel raised her right paw and felt Pinocchio's forehead.

"I'm afraid it's bad news," she sighed.

"What is it?"

"You do have a fever."

"What kind?"

"Donkey fever."

"I have no idea what you mean," said Pinocchio (who did).

"Allow me to explain, then," said the squirrel. "In two or three hours' time, you'll no longer be a puppet, still less a boy..."

"What will I be?"

"In two or three hours' time you'll be a donkey. A proper little donkey, like the ones that pull carts of cabbages and lettuces to market."

"Oh, poor me!" Pinocchio cried. He grabbed hold of his ears, yanking at them so furiously you'd have thought they weren't part of him at all.

"There's nothing to be done about it now, dear boy," the squirrel said, by way of consolation. "That's just the way it is. Any child who turns his back on books and schools and teachers and spends all day having fun will turn into a donkey sooner or later."

"It can't be true!" sobbed Pinocchio.

"It's the gospel truth, unfortunately, so there's no point in crying. You should have thought about it earlier."

"But it wasn't my fault," said Pinocchio. "It was Lampwick's."

"Who is Lampwick?"

"A friend of mine. I wanted to go home; I wanted to carry on studying and doing well at school, but Lampwick kept saying, 'Why do that boring schoolwork? Why go to school at all? Come to Toyland with me: we'll live the high life and never study again.'"

"And why did you take such bad advice?" the squirrel asked. "He doesn't sound like much of a friend."

"Because I'm an extremely silly and heartless puppet. If I weren't, I'd never have abandoned the kind fairy, who loved me like a mother. And by this time I wouldn't be a puppet any more – I'd be a nice, well-behaved boy like any other. Just wait till I get my hands on Lampwick! I'm going to give him a piece of my mind."

Pinocchio went to go outside. When he reached the front door, though, he remembered his donkey's ears, and was too ashamed to leave the house. He went back in and found a large cotton cap, which he pulled down over his ears all the way down to his nose.

Then he went out. He looked everywhere for Lampwick. He scoured the streets and visited all the puppet theatres, but without success. He asked everyone he met if they had seen him, but nobody had.

Finally he went to Lampwick's house. He knocked on the door.

"Who is it?" Lampwick's voice answered.

"It's me!" Pinocchio called.

"Wait a minute," Lampwick replied.

Half an hour later the door opened. Pinocchio was surprised to see his friend wearing a large cotton cap, pulled all the way down to his nose.

The sight of that cap suddenly raised Pinocchio's spirits. Could Lampwick have donkey fever as well?

The puppet pretended not to have noticed anything.

"How are you, my dear Lampwick?" he smiled.

"Never better," replied his friend. "Like a cat in a dairy."

"Are you sure?"

"Why shouldn't I be?"

"If you're so sure, why are you wearing that cap over your ears?"

"Doctor's orders," Lampwick replied. "I've bumped my knee. And what about you, my dear puppet? Why are you wearing a hat almost down to your nose?"

"Doctor's orders," said Pinocchio. "I grazed my foot."

"Poor Pinocchio!"

"Poor Lampwick!"

In the silence that followed, the two friends stared at each other, smirking.

Pinocchio was the first to speak.

"Lampwick," he said, "have you ever suffered from ear infections?"

"Never," replied Lampwick. "And yourself?"

"Never. Although this morning one of my ears does seem to be giving me a bit of trouble."

"Me too!"

"You too? And which ear is it?"

"Both of them. What about you?"

"Both of them," said Pinocchio. "Could it be the same disease?"

"I'm afraid it might be."

"Would you do me a favour, Lampwick?"

"Naturally."

"Would you show me your ears?"

"Of course. But first I want to see yours, my dear Pinocchio."

"No, no, you first."

"Not likely! You first. Then I'll show you mine."

"Let's behave like friends," said the puppet. "Friends compromise."

"What do you mean?"

"Let's take our hats off at the same time. Agreed?"

"Agreed."

Pinocchio began to count: "One, two, three..."

On the count of three, both boys pulled off their hats and threw them in the air.

What happened next might seem incredible, but it is absolutely true. When Pinocchio and Lampwick realized they shared the same predicament, instead of  feeling horrified and upset they began to wiggle their ludicrous ears and pull faces at each other, until they doubled up with laughter.

They laughed and laughed till their sides ached. Then, suddenly, Lampwick fell quiet. His face turned grey. He began to stagger.

"Help, Pinocchio!" he called out to his friend.

"What's wrong?"

"I can't stand up!"

"Neither can I!" Pinocchio wailed, almost falling over.

And as they spoke these words, they both fell to the floor and began to crawl around the room on their hands and knees. As they crawled, their hands turned into hooves, their faces lengthened into muzzles and their backs sprouted light-grey fur, speckled with black.

But the moment of deepest humiliation for our two unfortunate friends came when they felt their tails beginning to grow. Overcome with shame and sorrow, they opened their mouths to complain, but all they could produce were donkey's brays.

They were braying away in harmony, when a knock came at the door. "Open up! I am the coachman who brought you here. Open up this minute, or else!"

CHAPTER 33

When nobody answered the door, the coachman kicked it open.

"Congratulations, lads!" he said to Pinocchio and Lampwick with his usual honeyed smile. "First-class braying. I recognized your voices and came at once."

The two donkeys hung their heads, their ears drooping and their tails between their legs. At first the little man stroked and patted them. Then he pulled out a curry-comb and gave them a good grooming. When their coats shone like mirrors, he put halters over their heads and led them to market, where he planned to sell them and make a tidy profit.

There was no lack of buyers. Lampwick was sold to a farmer whose donkey had died the day before. Pinocchio was bought by a circus manager who wanted to train him to dance and perform tricks.

By now, my dear readers, you may have guessed what the coachman's game was. This horrid little monster, who looked as if butter wouldn't melt in his mouth, would regularly travel round the world luring lazy boys into his carriage. Once they were on board, he brought them to Toyland so that they could waste day after day having fun. Then, when indolence turned the poor things into donkeys, he took them to market. In this way he had become a millionaire in just a few years.

What happened to Lampwick after he was bought by the farmer, I do not know. What I do know is that for Pinocchio his sale at the market was the beginning of a harsh and miserable period in his life.

When his new owner took him to his stable, he filled the manger with straw. Pinocchio took one mouthful and spat it out.

Grumbling, the circus manager filled the manger with hay instead. The donkey spat that out too.

"So my hay's not good enough for you either?" the manager shouted angrily. And he struck Pinocchio across the legs with his whip.

"Hee-haw, hee-haw, I can't digest straw," the poor donkey brayed.

"Eat hay, then," replied his owner, who understood donkey language perfectly.

"Hee-haw, hee-haw, hay makes my tummy sore."

"What do you expect – breast of capon and chicken galantine?" his owner raged, giving him another taste of the whip.

After that Pinocchio thought it safest to hold his tongue.

The circus manager left the stable, bolting the door behind him. Pinocchio was alone. He hadn't eaten anything for a very long time, and he began to yawn with hunger. His mouth opened as wide as an oven. In the end, as there was nothing else in the manger, he took a mouthful of the hay. After chewing on it for a long time, he closed his eyes and swallowed.

"It could be worse, I suppose," he said to himself. "But how I wish I'd stayed at school. I'd be eating a nice ham sandwich instead."

When Pinocchio woke the following morning he looked around for more hay, but he'd finished it all the night before. He took a mouthful of straw. It wasn't exactly mushroom risotto or spaghetti with tomato sauce.

"Never mind," he sighed, "I just hope my story will be a lesson to others who'd rather skive than study." And he sighed again.

"What are you sighing about?" shouted his master, bursting through the stable door. "Do you think I paid good money to watch you stand around eating all day? You've got work to do, my lad. You're going to earn your keep. Come on, we're going to the big tent. I'm going to teach you to jump through paper hoops," he said, "and to waltz. And to do the polka on your hind legs."

Poor Pinocchio had no choice. He did eventually master these fine arts, but only after many months of lessons and many a blow of the whip.

At last the day came when the circus manager was able to announce a grand performance, with Pinocchio as the main attraction. Big posters on every street corner read:

GRAND PERFORMANCE

TONIGHT!

acROBaTiCs AND FEATS OF DARING!

performed by

ARTISTS and HORSES OF BOTH SEXES!

AND INTRODUCING the LEGENDARY

Little DONKEY PINOCCHIO

also Known as

STAR OF the DANCE!

* * * * *

FULL LIGHTING THROUGHOUT

That evening the big top was full to overflowing an hour before the show began. The ringside seats were teeming with girls and boys of every age and size who couldn't wait to see the legendary Little Donkey Pinocchio.

Towards the end of the show, the circus manager stepped into the ring, dressed in a black jacket, white breeches and leather riding boots. He gave a low bow.

"Ladies and gentlemen, girls and boys," he said with great solemnity. "The humble undersigned – being at the present time in perambulation through this illustrious metropolis – is desirous to grant himself the privilege, indeed the pleasure, of presenting to this intelligent and distinguished audience a celebrated donkey, which has already had the honour of performing in the presence of Their Majesties the Emperors of all the principal courts of Europe.

"Thank you for your attention, ladies and gentlemen. Let me now beg you to cast your most approbatory eye on this act of indubitable verisimilitude, and to forgive our humble establishment for any eventual inadequacy."

This preposterous speech was greeted with gales of laughter and loud applause, which grew into a hurricane when Pinocchio himself appeared. He was the last word in donkey elegance. He had a new halter of shiny leather, with brass buckles and studs and a white camellia at each ear. His mane was divided into dozens of little curls, tied up with red bows. There was a broad gold-and-silver sash round his waist, and his tail was plaited with crimson-and-blue ribbons. In short, he looked adorable.

"Ladies and gentlemen!" the manager declared. "Will I waste your precious time with tall stories about my intrepid efforts to capture and subdue this mammal, as it roamed freely from mountain to mountain on the great equatorial plains of the equator? I will not. Will I invite you to observe the savage light in its eyes? I will. Picture your humble servant applying all methods of domestication and failing. Time and again I was forced to resort to the subtle articulacy of the whip. But all such kindness, far from soothing the savage beast, merely enraged it further, until at long last your humble servant located in the beast's cranium a small cartilaginous area, which the Medical Faculty of Paris declares to be the section of the brain which governs hair growth and ballroom dancing. I therefore elected to train the quadruped in the noble art of dancing and jumping through paper-covered hoops. Ladies and gentlemen, boys and girls, judge for yourselves the efficacy of my labours! But before commencing the performance," the circus master continued, "please allow me to announce that in the event of bad weather, tomorrow evening's show will be brought forward to tomorrow morning, at the hour of eleven o'clock pm."

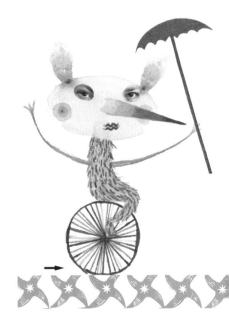

The ringmaster concluded with another bow, then turned to his star.

"Greet the ladies and gentlemen, Pinocchio," he ordered.

Pinocchio obediently bent his front legs until he was kneeling. He stayed down until the manager, cracking his whip, barked, "Walk!"

The donkey stood up and began to walk around the ring.

"Trot!" the manager cried. Pinocchio quickened his pace.

"Canter!" ordered the manager. Pinocchio obeyed.

"Gallop!" came the final command, and Pinocchio began to gallop flat out. As he was careering around the ring at top speed, the manager fired a pistol shot into the air and Pinocchio fell to the floor, pretending to be wounded. The audience clapped, shouted and whistled so loudly, it's a wonder they didn't bring the roof down.

As Pinocchio scrambled to his feet, he looked up into the crowd and spotted a beautiful lady wearing a gold chain around her neck. On the end of this chain was a medallion. On the medallion was a painted portrait of a wooden puppet.

"That's me! That lady's my fairy!" Pinocchio realized, recognizing her at once. Overcome with joy, he tried to call her by name, but all that he could produce was a "hee-haw", so long and so loud that the whole audience – particularly the children – burst into peals of laughter. The manager, annoyed, rapped Pinocchio smartly on the nose with the handle of his whip, to teach him that it is not good manners to bray at your public. The poor donkey stuck his tongue out and licked his nose for at least five minutes, hoping perhaps to wash the pain away.

When he looked into the audience again, the fairy's seat was empty.

Tears filled Pinocchio's eyes and rolled down his furry cheeks, but nobody noticed, least of all the manager. He cracked his whip and cried, "Come on, Pinocchio, show these ladies and gentlemen how gracefully you jump through a hoop."

Pinocchio tried two or three times, but each time he came to the hoop he found it preferable to pass underneath it. In the end he did jump, and got through,

but his hind legs got caught in the hoop, and he landed in a heap on the other side.

When he stood up again he was limping so badly that he was barely able to get back to his stable.

"We want Pinocchio, we want Pinocchio!" chanted the children, who felt sorry for the donkey. But he did not return to the ring that evening.

The next morning the horse doctor came to see him, and declared that he would be lame for the rest of his life.

"What use is a lame donkey? It's just another mouth to feed," the manager told the stable boy. "You'd better take him back to market."

When Pinocchio and the stable boy arrived at the market, a buyer approached them straight away.

"How much for this lame donkey?" he asked.

"Twenty guineas."

"I'll give you twenty farthings," the buyer offered. "I'm not buying him to work for me, only for his hide. It looks nice and thick – just right to make a drum skin for my village band."

When the buyer had handed over the twenty farthings, he led the donkey to a low cliff by the seashore. He tied a rock round Pinocchio's neck and attached a long rope to one hind leg. Then he gave him a sudden shove so that he fell into the sea.

Pinocchio sank straight to the bottom. His new owner, holding on tight to the rope, settled down comfortably and waited for him to drown.

CHaPTER 34

"My poor lame donkey must be drowned by now," Pinocchio's master said to himself when the donkey had been underwater for fifty minutes. "It's time to pull him up and start making that drum."

He began to pull on the rope that he'd tied to Pinocchio's leg. He pulled and pulled, until at last he saw something appear on the surface of the water.

Instead of the dead donkey he'd expected, Pinocchio's new owner saw a live puppet, squirming like an eel. The poor man thought he must be dreaming. He stood there gaping at Pinocchio with his eyes popping out of his head.

Once he had recovered a little, he gibbered, "But where ... where is the donkey ... the one I pushed in the water?"

"It's me!" the puppet replied, laughing.

"You?"

"Me," Pinocchio confirmed.

"You're trying to make me look stupid, you scoundrel!"

"Far from it, master. I'm absolutely serious."

"But how did you turn into a puppet?"

"It must have been the sea water. It can play strange tricks."

"Watch it, puppet – don't think you can take me for a ride."

"Untie my leg for me," Pinocchio ventured, "and I'll tell you how it happened."

The new owner was curious. He loosened the rope. Pinocchio, free at last, began to tell his tale.

"Before I was a donkey, I was a puppet, just like I am now," he explained. "I was even very close to becoming a real boy. But I was lazy and I couldn't be bothered to study. I listened to Bad Influences and ran away from home. Then one day I woke up and found I'd turned into a donkey, with donkey ears and a donkey tail. I was so ashamed. It was terrible. I wouldn't wish that on anybody – even you.

"Then I got taken to market and sold to a circus manager. He said he'd turn me into a great dancer and acrobat. But I had a bad fall, and I ended up lame in both legs. My master sent me back to market, and that was how you came to buy me."

"Yes," interrupted the man, "and I paid twenty farthings for you. How am I going to get that back now?"

"But why did you buy me?" Pinocchio asked in outrage. "To make a drum skin out of me! A drum skin!"

"Yes," complained the man, "and where am I going to find another drum skin now?"

"Don't worry, master," Pinocchio said. "I'm sure you'll find another donkey."

"You cheeky beggar," said the man. "Is that the end of your story?"

"No," replied the puppet. "There's a little more. After you'd bought me, you brought me here to kill me. But then you decided instead to tie a stone around my neck and throw me into the sea. But unluckily for you, master, you reckoned without the fairy..."

"And who might she be?"

"She's my mother, and like all loving mothers she never lets her child out of her sight. She gets him out of trouble even when he's behaved so badly that he doesn't deserve it. So anyway, as I was saying, when my beloved fairy saw that I was about to drown, she sent a huge school of fish who thought I really was a poor dead donkey and began to eat me. And how they ate! I never would have believed that fish could be greedier than children. Some ate my ears; some ate my muzzle, neck and mane. Some ate the skin off my legs and the fur off my back... One little fish was kind enough to gobble up the whole of my tail."

"Good grief!" exclaimed the buyer. "That's the last time I eat fish. Imagine tucking into a nice mullet and finding a donkey's tail inside!"

"Quite," laughed the puppet. "Anyway, once the fish had eaten their way through the outer layers of donkey, they naturally reached the bone – or, in my case, the wood. (As you can see, that's what I'm made of: high-quality hardwood.) But it only took a few nibbles for them to realize that wood wasn't to their taste, and then off they swam, without so much as a thank you. And there you are: that's why you ended up with a puppet on your rope."

"I couldn't care less how you got here!" Pinocchio's owner suddenly exploded. "All I know is that I spent twenty farthings on you, and I want them back! I know what I'll do," he decided. "I'll take you back to market and sell you off as kindling."

"Please yourself," said Pinocchio, as he dived headlong into the sea.

"Goodbye," he shouted back to the unfortunate new owner. "Remember me, next time you feel like making a drum."

He laughed and swam on. After a while he turned back again, and yelled even louder, "Goodbye again. Remember me, next time you need kindling."

In the twinkling of an eye he'd swum so far that you could hardly see him from the shore. He was no more than a little dot on the surface of the sea – a dot which occasionally leapt out of the water and turned a somersault, like a dolphin in high spirits.

As Pinocchio was swimming along, not caring where he was going, he spotted a rock that looked like white marble, sticking out of the water. On top of this rock stood a pretty little goat. She was bleating at Pinocchio and beckoning with one of her front legs, imploring him to come closer. This was strange enough, but the strangest thing of all was that the goat's fleece wasn't white, or black, or even a mixture of the two, like that of other goats. It was blue, a wonderfully bright blue, which reminded the puppet of his beloved fairy's hair.

Pinocchio's heart began to beat faster. He set off towards the white rock with renewed energy. He was halfway there, when a sea-monster's ghastly head rose out of the water and came rushing towards him.

The gaping chasm of its enormous mouth was framed by three rows of fangs, which would have made the stoutest of hearts miss a beat. It was none other than the merciless shark that has been mentioned more than once in this story. Through its terrible deeds, it had come to be known as "Attila, the scourge of fishermen".

The terrified Pinocchio tried to swim out of the path of the huge gaping mouth, but it followed him at the speed of an arrow.

"Hurry, for heaven's sake!" bleated the goat. Pinocchio swam as fast as he could.

"Swim, Pinocchio, it's getting closer!" the goat bleated again.

Pinocchio summoned every ounce of strength in his body and managed to double his speed.

"It's right behind you, Pinocchio!" the goat bleated a third time. "Faster, faster, or you're lost!"

Pinocchio sped along like a bullet ... he was almost at the rock ... the goat was stretching out her front legs to help him from the water... But it was too late. The shark caught up with him and sucked him into its mouth, like a child sucking a strand of spaghetti. The monster swallowed so fiercely and greedily that Pinocchio landed in its stomach with a tremendous thump. He lay there for a while, unconscious.

When he came to, he had no idea where he was. It was pitch-black – so dark that he felt as if he'd plunged his head into a bottle of black ink. He listened but could hear no sound. His only sensation was a strong gust of wind that buffeted him at regular intervals. At first he couldn't work out where it could be coming from, but then he realized it must come from the creature's lungs. (The shark had dreadful asthma.

When it breathed, it was like a force-ten gale.)

At first Pinocchio managed to keep his spirits up. Then, as everything around him confirmed that he was trapped inside a sea-monster's body, he began to sob and scream.

"Help!" he wailed. "Help! Will nobody come and save me?"

"You'll be lucky," commented a voice that sounded like an out-of-tune guitar.

"Who's that?" asked Pinocchio, cold with fear.

"It's just me, a poor tuna who's been swallowed by the shark, like you have," replied the voice. "What kind of fish are you?"

"I'm not a fish, I'm a puppet."

"Then why did you get yourself swallowed by a shark?"

"I didn't do it on purpose. Anyway, what are we going to do now?"

"Resign ourselves to our fate, and wait for the shark to digest us."

"But I don't want to be digested!" Pinocchio howled, beginning to cry again.

"You're not the only one," said the fish. "But I try to be philosophical and tell myself that, for a tuna, it's more dignified to die in water than in sunflower oil."

"That's stupid!" Pinocchio yelled.

"Well it happens to be my view," the tuna-fish replied, "and views, as our tuna leaders are fond of remarking, should be respected."

"I want to get out. I want to escape..."

"Go on, then, escape if you can."

"Is this shark really so big?" Pinocchio asked.

"More than a mile long," replied the fish. "*Without* his tail."

While they were talking in the darkness, Pinocchio thought he saw a glimmer of light very far away.

"What's that light over there?" he asked.

"Some other poor wretch waiting to be digested, I expect," said the tuna.

"I'll go and find him. He may be a wise old fish who'll direct me to the exit."

"I sincerely hope so, dear puppet."

"Goodbye, tuna."

"Goodbye, puppet, and good luck."

"Will we meet again?"

"Who knows?" said the tuna. "Better not to dwell on such thoughts."

Chapter 35

Pinocchio advanced, step by step, towards the pinprick of light, groping his way through the merciless shark's body in the darkness.

As he walked he could feel his feet splashing through a puddle of slippery, oily liquid, which smelt so strongly of fried hake that he could have been in a fish-and-chip shop.

The further he got, the clearer the light became until, after walking and walking, he arrived. And do you know what he found?

I bet you'll never guess, not in a million years...

He found a small table, laid for dinner. It was lit by a candle stuck in a green bottle. Sitting at the table was an old man, so heavily covered in white hair that he could have been made out of snow or whipped cream. He was eating – slowly and without much enthusiasm – a dish of live fish: so very live that sometimes they jumped out of his mouth as he ate.

Pinocchio suddenly felt so happy that he almost fainted. He wanted to laugh; he wanted to cry. He wanted to say a thousand things. For a long while, though, all he could do was stammer incoherently. At last he managed a yell of joy. Opening his arms wide, he flung them round the old man's neck.

"Father!" he yelled. "I've found you at last! I won't ever leave you again, ever!"

"So it really is true?" said the old man, rubbing his eyes. "It's really you, Pinocchio?"

"Yes," Pinocchio laughed. "It's really me! And you've already forgiven me, haven't you? Oh, how good and kind you are, Father! And to think that I... Oh, if you only knew the things I've been through – the trouble I've had! The day you sold your jacket to buy my copybook, I ran away to see the puppet show, and the puppet-master wanted to throw me on the fire, but then he gave me five gold coins to bring to you, and I met a fox and a cat, who took me to the Red Lobster Inn, and when I set off again some assassins hanged me on a branch of the Great Oak and the pretty blue-haired girl sent for me with a carriage, and the doctors visited me and said, 'If he's not dead, he must be alive.' Then I told a lie, and my nose grew so long I couldn't get it out of the bedroom door, so then the fox and the cat came with me to bury the four gold coins, and a parrot laughed at me, and instead of two thousand coins I found nothing at all, and then the judge threw me into prison. And when I got out again I got caught in a trap and the farmer put a dog-collar on me so that I'd guard the henhouse, but then he realized I was innocent and let me go, and the snake with a smoking tail laughed so much that he burst a vein in his chest, and I got back to the girl's house, but she was dead and the dove said he'd seen you building a boat to go and look for me, and I said, 'I wish I had wings!' and he said, 'Do you want to go to your father?' and I said, 'Of course! But how?' and he said, 'I'll take you on my back,' and we flew all through the night, and then, the next day, some fishermen said there was a poor man in a boat, who was about to drown, and my heart told me it was you, although you were too far off to see, and I waved at you to come back to shore..."

"I recognized you, too," Geppetto interrupted, "and I wanted to come back to you, but the sea was too rough. Then my boat capsized and this massive shark swam straight at me. He caught me on his tongue and gobbled me up like a fairy cake."

"How long have you been here?" Pinocchio asked.

"About two years," replied his father. "Although it's felt more like two centuries."

"How have you kept alive?" Pinocchio asked. "Where did you find that candle? And matches to light it?"

"Let me tell you the whole story," said Geppetto. "The same storm that capsized my little boat sank a large merchant ship. The sailors were all rescued, but the ship went straight to the bottom, and the shark, who was feeling peckish, swallowed it up."

"What, all in one go?" Pinocchio cried.

"All in one go. The only thing he spat out was the main mast, because it got stuck between his teeth like a fish bone. Luckily for me, the ship was full of useful things: tins of corned beef, biscuits, bottles of wine, raisins, cheese, coffee, sugar, candles, matches ... enough for these two years. But now there's nothing left in the storeroom. This is my last candle."

"And when it's burned down?" Pinocchio asked.

"When this one's burned down, my child, we'll be in the dark."

"Then there's no time to lose," said Pinocchio. "We've got to escape."

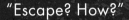

"Escape? How?"

"We'll climb out of the shark's mouth and jump into the sea."

"Excellent idea, my boy. Or it would be, if I could swim."

"That doesn't matter: I'll take you on my back. I'm a strong swimmer – I can get you to land safe and sound."

Geppetto shook his head and smiled sadly.

"Wishful thinking, my boy. Do you really believe that a little puppet could swim all that way with a man on his back?"

"Try me," said Pinocchio. "In any case, if it's written in the stars that we're doomed, at least we'll die in each other's arms."

To cut the argument short, Pinocchio took the candle off the table and held it up so that it lit the way ahead.

"Follow me, Father," he said. "And don't be afraid."

They walked the length of the shark's body. When they reached his throat, they decided to stop for a minute to look around and choose the best moment for their escape.

Now you should know that the merciless shark – being elderly and prone to asthma and palpitations of the heart – was forced to sleep with his mouth wide open. This meant that when Pinocchio peered up his throat he could see a beautiful moonlit night and a large expanse of starry sky.

"Perfect timing," he whispered to his father. "The shark is fast asleep. It's as bright as day. The sea is calm. Follow me and we'll be free in no time."

Up the sea-monster's throat they clambered, and when they reached its cavernous mouth they tiptoed carefully along its tongue, which was as long and wide as a good-sized garden path. They were on the verge of jumping into the sea when the shark suddenly sneezed so violently that Pinocchio and Geppetto were blown off their feet and thrown right back into the monster's stomach.

Their candle was extinguished in the fall, and father and son were left in the dark.

"Now what?" Pinocchio wondered aloud.

"Now," his father answered, "we're done for."

"Done for? Nonsense!" Pinocchio said. "Give me your hand, Father, and watch you don't slip."

"Where are we going?"

"We have to try again. Follow me and don't be afraid."

Pinocchio took his father by the hand and they tiptoed back up the monster's throat. This time they managed to walk the length of the tongue and clamber over the three rows of teeth.

Before braving the leap into the sea, Pinocchio turned to his father.

"Climb onto my back and hold on tight. I'll do the rest," he said.

As soon as Geppetto was settled comfortably on his son's back, Pinocchio dived confidently into the water and began to swim. The sea was as flat as a millpond. The moon shone in all its splendour, and the merciless shark was still so fast asleep that ten cannons wouldn't have woken it.

CHAPTER 36

Pinocchio swam as fast as he could towards the shore. As he swam, he noticed that his father (who was riding on the puppet's back with his legs trailing in the water) was shivering all over, as if he had a temperature. Was it the cold, or was it fear? Both, perhaps. Pinocchio took it to be fear, and tried to rally the old man's spirits.

"Don't worry, Father. We'll be on dry land in a few minutes," he said.

"But where is this blessed land?" Geppetto asked. He was growing more and more anxious, peering at the horizon like a tailor squinting through the eye of a needle. "All I can see is sky and water."

"Well, I can see land," said the puppet. "I'm like a cat – I see better at night."

Pinocchio was putting on a brave face, but the truth was that he was beginning to feel uneasy. His strength was waning. He was panting heavily. In short, he was close to collapse – and the beach was still a long way off.

He swam on for as long as he could, then he looked up at Geppetto and stammered, "Help ... I can't go on ... I'm dying."

Father and son were about to drown.

Then they heard a voice that sounded like an out-of-tune guitar.

"Dying?" it asked. "Who's dying?"

"My father," Pinocchio gasped, "and me."

"I recognize that voice. It's Pinocchio, isn't it?"

"That's right," said Pinocchio. "Who are you?"

"I'm the tuna-fish – your fellow-prisoner in the belly of the shark."

"How did you get out?"

"The same way as you," the tuna replied. "I watched you and escaped just after you did."

"Tuna, my friend, you've arrived in the nick of time!" Pinocchio cried. "Please, for the love of your tuna-children, save us, or we're lost."

"Of course! Hang onto my tail, both of you, and let me pull you. We'll be at the beach in four minutes."

Geppetto and Pinocchio didn't need to be asked twice, although they decided it was more comfortable to sit on the fish's back than to hold onto his tail.

"Are we too heavy?" Pinocchio asked.

"Heavy? You're as light as seashells," replied the tuna, who was a big strong fish the size of a two-year-old calf.

When they reached the shore Pinocchio jumped down first to help his father. Then he turned back to the tuna.

"My dearest friend," he said in a trembling voice. "You saved my father's life! I'll never be able to thank you enough. Can I at least give you a kiss?"

The fish stuck his head out of the water and Pinocchio knelt down and kissed him on the lips.

This spontaneous show of affection so moved the fish (who was unused to such things) that he sank back underwater and swam off quickly, embarrassed to be seen crying like a baby.

Meanwhile, the sun had come up.

Geppetto was so weak he was barely able to stand. Pinocchio offered him his arm. "Lean on me, Father," he said, "and let's be on our way. We'll creep along like snails and stop whenever we get tired."

"But where are we going?" asked Geppetto.

"To look for a house ... a hut ... a hovel – anywhere where they might give us a bite to eat and some straw to sleep on," replied his son.

They'd walked less than fifty metres when they passed two shady-looking characters who were begging by the side of the road. It was the cat and the fox, but they were so changed that Pinocchio barely recognized them. The cat had spent so long pretending to be blind that he'd ended up losing his sight. The fox was paralyzed down one side of his body and was old and weatherbeaten. He'd even lost his beautiful tail, which he'd been forced to sell for a fly-swat.

"Dear Pinocchio," the fox whined, "spare a penny for two miserable invalids."

"...serable invalids," echoed the cat.

"You fooled me once, you ruffians. You're not doing it again. Goodbye," replied Pinocchio.

"But Pinocchio," said the fox, "this time we really are desperate."

"...desperate," echoed the cat.

"Serves you right," the puppet replied. "Remember the wise old saying, 'You made your bed – you'll have to lie on it.' Goodbye."

"Take pity on us!" whined the fox.

"...us!" echoed the cat.

"Reap as ye have sown," replied Pinocchio. "Goodbye."

"Don't desert us!" whined the fox.

"...us!" came the echo.

"The devil's flour is all bran," replied the puppet. "Goodbye."

And with these words Pinocchio and Geppetto went on their way. A hundred yards further on they saw, at the end of a path through the fields, a handsome cabin with straw walls and a tiled roof.

"Let's knock at the door," Pinocchio said.

So they did.

"Who is it?" asked a little voice from inside.

"A father and son," the puppet answered, "looking for food and shelter."

"Turn the key and the door will open."

Pinocchio turned the key and the door opened. The two of them walked in and looked around, but they couldn't see anybody.

"Where's the owner gone?" Pinocchio said, surprised.

"I'm up here," called the voice.

Father and son looked up to the ceiling. There, on a beam, was the talking cricket.

"It's my friend!" Pinocchio cried. "What a pleasure to see you," he added, bowing politely.

"It's a pleasure now, is it?" said the insect. "Last time you saw me, you threw a mallet at me."

"I know, I know," Pinocchio said miserably. "Send me away ... throw a mallet at me if you want to. But please, please help my poor father."

"I'll help you both," said the cricket. "I reminded you of your rudeness merely to demonstrate that you should always be polite and helpful, if you can – because, one day, you may be the one in need."

"You're right, cricket, you're absolutely right," said Pinocchio apologetically. "I'll never be so rude and unpleasant again. But tell me, how did you manage to buy this lovely hut?"

"I didn't buy it – it was given to me. Yesterday; by a pretty little goat with the most beautiful blue fleece."

"Where did she go?" Pinocchio cried eagerly.

"I'm afraid I don't know," the cricket replied.

"When is she coming back?"

"I don't think she is. She left looking terribly sad. She was bleating, 'Poor Pinocchio, I'm never going to see him again ... he'll be deep inside the shark by now.'"

"So it was her!" wailed Pinocchio, bursting into tears.

When he'd finished sobbing, he dried his eyes and made up a comfortable straw bed for Geppetto. Then he asked the cricket, "Tell me, where can I get my father a glass of milk?"

"Giangio, the greengrocer, lives three fields away. He keeps cows, so you should be able to get some there."

Pinocchio ran all the way.

"How much milk do you want?" the greengrocer asked.

"One glassful, please," replied Pinocchio.

"One glass of milk costs a penny, so hand it over."

"But I don't have a penny," Pinocchio said sadly.

"If you don't have a penny, Mr Puppet, I don't have any milk."

"Oh well, never mind," Pinocchio sighed, turning to go.

"Wait a minute," said Giangio. "I'm sure we can come to an arrangement. Do you think you could work my windlass?"

"What's a windlass?"

"It's a machine that draws water from the well. I use it to water my vegetables."

"I'll try..."

"Draw a hundred buckets and I'll give you a glass of milk."

"All right," agreed Pinocchio. So Giangio took the puppet to the vegetable garden and showed him how to turn the windlass. Pinocchio set to work, but long before he'd drawn a hundred buckets he was aching in every limb. He'd never worked so hard in his life.

"My donkey used to do this for me," said the greengrocer, "but now he's so ill I think he's going to die."

"May I see him?" asked Pinocchio.

"Of course."

When Pinocchio walked into the stable he saw a donkey lying on the straw, worn out by hunger and overwork.

I'm sure I know this donkey, he thought, beginning to tremble.

He bent down closer and asked, in donkey language, "Who are you?"

The donkey opened his tired eyes and stammered, "I'm ... Lam ... Lamp..."

With that, he closed his eyes and died.

"Oh, my poor Lampwick!" Pinocchio whispered. He picked up a handful of straw and used it to wipe away a tear.

"Imagine how I feel," said Giangio. "I spent good money on him!"

"He was a ... friend of mine," said Pinocchio.

"A friend of yours?"

"A classmate."

"You had donkeys in your class?" Giangio hooted with laughter. "That must have been a good school!"

Pinocchio was too ashamed to answer. He took his glass of warm milk and went back to the cricket's house.

From that day onwards, for more than five months, Pinocchio got up before dawn each day to go and earn the glass of milk that was such a tonic for his ailing father. And that was not all: in his spare time he taught himself to weave baskets from rushes. By selling them he was able to provide for all household expenses. He also built, with his own hands, a fine wheelchair to take his father out for a breath of fresh air on sunny days.

In the evenings, Pinocchio practised his reading and writing. In the nearby town he had bought, for just a few pence, a large book that was missing its title page and index but was excellent for reading practice. For writing, he used a sharpened twig which, since he had no ink or inkwell, he dipped into a mixture of cherry and blackberry juice.

Such was the effort and ingenuity he put into caring for his father that he managed not only to make the old man really quite comfortable, but also to put aside forty coins to buy some new clothes for himself.

"I'm off to the market," he said to Geppetto one morning. "I'm going to buy a new jacket, a hat and a pair of shoes. When I get home you won't recognize me," he laughed.

He left the hut and set off towards the town, a spring in his step. All of a sudden he heard someone calling him by name. Turning round, he saw a fine-looking snail peeping out of the hedgerow.

"Don't you recognize me?" the snail asked.

"I'm not sure..."

"Don't you remember the snail who was the blue-haired fairy's maid? Don't you remember the time I came downstairs to let you into her house, and you got your foot stuck in the door?"

"I do remember! I remember it all!" cried Pinocchio. "Where is the fairy? Do tell me, dear snail. What is she doing? Has she forgiven me? Does she remember me? Does she still love me? Is she far from here? Can I go and see her?"

The snail endured this breathless questioning with her usual calm.

"Pinocchio, my child," she said at last, "the fairy is in hospital."

"Hospital?"

"I'm afraid so. She fell on hard times. Now she is seriously ill and hasn't a penny to her name."

"What terrible news!" cried Pinocchio. "Poor, poor fairy! I wish I had a million gold pieces to give her, but I've only got forty coins. I was just off to buy some clothes. Here, take the money. Get it to my fairy as quick as you can."

"But what about your new clothes?"

"I'd sell these rags I'm wearing if I thought it would help. Go to her, dear snail – hurry! Come back here in two days' time: I should be able to give you something more. If I can work to keep my father, I can work five hours more to keep my darling mother as well. Goodbye, snail. Remember to come back!"

The snail, so slow by nature, sped off as fast as a lizard under the August sun.

When Pinocchio got back home, his father asked about his new clothes.

"Nothing would fit," Pinocchio replied. "Never mind! I'll buy them another time."

That evening, instead of working until ten o'clock Pinocchio carried on till after midnight. Instead of making his usual eight baskets, he made sixteen. Then he went to bed and fell asleep. He dreamt of his beloved blue fairy, looking radiant and happy.

"Well done, Pinocchio!" she said, kissing him. "Your heart is so good, I forgive you all your mischief. Children who care for their aging parents with affection deserve our love and praise, even if they aren't always good. Carry on like this, and you'll be happy."

The dream ended, and Pinocchio sat bolt upright in bed.

It was then that he realized (just imagine his amazement!) that he wasn't a wooden puppet any longer. He had turned into a real boy. He looked around. Instead of the familiar straw walls of the hut, he saw a pretty little bedroom, furnished and decorated with elegant simplicity. Jumping down from the bed, he found a brand-new set of clothes, a new hat and a pair of leather boots that suited him perfectly.

Once he was dressed, he put his hands in his pockets. In one of them he found a small ivory purse, on which were carved these words:

The BLUE FAiRY RETURNS the FORTY coins to her BELOVED PINOCCHIO, and THANKS HIM for HiS KINDNESS.

When he opened the purse he found, instead of his forty copper coins, forty shining new gold coins.

Pinocchio went to the mirror. He didn't recognize his reflection. It was no longer the wooden puppet he knew so well, but the lively, intelligent face of a handsome boy with brown hair, blue eyes and a merry, laughing expression.

Pinocchio no longer knew if he was awake or dreaming.

"Where's my father?" he cried suddenly. He rushed next door and found Geppetto looking healthy and cheerful, the way he used to. The carpenter had gone back to his craft and was in the process of making an ornate picture

frame, decorated with beautiful flowers, leaves and animal heads.

"Who worked all this magic, Father?" Pinocchio asked, once he'd jumped onto the old man's lap and smothered him with kisses.

"You," Geppetto answered.

"Why me?"

"Because when children finally decide to stop being naughty, and start behaving well, the whole family changes for the better."

"I wonder where the old Pinocchio has got to?"

"Look over there," Geppetto replied. He pointed to a large wooden puppet slumped against a chair. Its head was nodding to one side. Its arms were dangling uselessly. Its crossed legs were so very bent that it was a miracle it could stand up at all.

Pinocchio stared at his former self for a long while.

"How funny it was to be made of wood," he said to himself at last, "and how splendid it is to be real!"

q

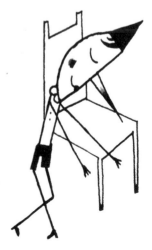